MESSAGES
FROM THE
HEART

by Edwin Allen Lee

ISBN 0-75964-062-9

This book is printed on acid free paper.

Published by 1st Books
in cooperation with Wino Publishing

DEDICATED TO THE LADIES
WHO HAVE IMPACTED MY LIFE
AND WRITING

MY NIECE & LITTLE BUDDY EVON SATCHER

PAT HOBAN

NANCY SAN CARLOS

DONNA BETHERS

MARSHA DRAKE

LUCY LEU

SHERI,

and, of course,

CISSY

CONTENTS

Other books by Edwin Allen Lee & James Fogle
> **Cissy's Magic** *by Fogle & Lee*
> **Happy Face Killer** *by Fogle & Lee*

Upcoming books from Wino Publishing
> **Purgation** *by Edwin Allen Lee*
> **Six Pack** *by Edwin Allen Lee*
> **In God's Eye** *by Edwin Allen Lee*
> **Division of Blood** *by Edwin Allen Lee*
> **The Franke Conspiracy** *by Edwin Allen Lee*
> **The Executive** *by Edwin Allen Lee*
> **The Zook Book** *by Stanley C. Zook*
> *A Cookbook for Full-figured Food Fanatics*
> **A Little left of Nowhere** *by Larry Breeden*
> **Albers File #1** *by Jerry Albers*
> *Captive Artist*
> **Albers File #2** *by Jerry Albers*
> *Outlaw Adventures*
> **Albers File #3** *by Jerry Albers*
> *Whitley vs Albers-The real truth behind the Oregon Sate Penetentiary's A-Block Bloodbath*

INTRODUCTION

Many events led me to write this book. Three powerful memories come to mind; events that left me breathless and in confusion. No, not the prison riots I've experienced, not the violent deaths I've seen, and definitely, not any of the false rehabilitation that the Department of Corrections may claim. Those breathless memories are; the death of my son Kent, being reunited with my daughter Cissy, and the words of a little nine year old girl when she came out from under anesthesia after a cancerous brain tumor operation.

She opened her eyes and smiled and said,

"Hi, Uncle Duke. How long have you been here anyway?"

So, Kent's Daddy, Cissy's Father and my little buddy Evon Satcher's Uncle Duke wrote this book, and often in tears.

Robert Frost once said,

"No tears in the writer, no tears in the reader."

My dear friend and nonviolent communicator, Lucy Leu, says my writing has proven Frost to be right.

Now, with great anticipation I await your opinion of my work. Thank you.

Respectfully,
Edward Allen Lee

ENVY

To the man coming home from a hard days work, in a pickup with fifteen payments left on it, that is ready to break down, with less than ten dollars in his pocket; to a chicken noodle soup dinner made by a wife who's a bit overweight, who has unkempt hair, is smelling of laundry soap and may have bad breath, with a house full of screaming kids playing in a toy-littered house; from the prison cell from which I'm writing this in one sentence, I say,

"God, How I **ENVY** You."

RACHAEL—THE AUTHOR—CISSY
SHORTLY BEFORE THEY WERE SEPARATED

MEMORIES OF BOMBEE

In 1971, I married a beautiful young lady named Sherrie. As a result of that marriage, my only daughter, Shirley Ann, was born. She was soon nick-named by me as "Cissy." Cissy became my best buddy as well. When she was old enough to start talking, I became her "Bombee." Every other father in the neighborhood was either Dad or Daddy, but I had to be Bombee.

When I entered the house after work, she would squeal "Bombeeee" as she ran up to me on fat little legs. It didn't take Cissy too long to find out that a sad sounding "Bombeeee" was all it took to escape taking her nap or getting her wish. I'll admit it; Cissy had her Bombee wrapped around her fat little finger.

When Cissy was little more than two years old, my parole was violated and I was sent back to prison. My wife filed for a divorce and I lost my little buddy. These are memories of terrible heartache.

Over the years, memories of big eyes, pigtails, short fat little legs, and a tiny voice calling "Bombeeee" often brought me tears and prayers. I would pray that my little buddy was safe, loved, and understood, wherever she was; and that whoever her new stepfather was, he would be a kind, loving, and understanding person. God...How I loved and missed my little buddy. That's a sad memory.

3

As the years passed, I was to survive three major prison riots. "A prison blood bath," was what one of them was called in the newspapers. Those memories, I'll never forget.

I once fought an exhibition fight with a top ten ranked heavyweight contender from Seattle. He pounded some memories into me that I'll not soon forget. But he never did knock me off my feet. I guess I'm kind of proud of that fact. Those are violent memories.

A couple years ago, I was on a national television program called 48 Hours, as a spokesman for the transitional release of prison inmates. Because it was one of those well-known network news programs, they sent a famous commentator to interview me for over ten hours just to get 42 minutes of tape. The commentator had bad breath. They make you sit real close on TV, you know. He didn't have any lenses in his glasses either. When I asked about his glasses, he said they were called "props" in television language. I told him they were called "phony" in convict language. He laughed to cover his embarrassment.

Prisoners learn to do that too, you know; laugh when their feelings are hurt. After the program aired, I got many visitors. All it took to see me was a call to the Assistant Superintendent saying they had seen me on TV, and the visit would be cleared. Most of the people who came to see me were media types. Some were even kind of famous locally. They all seemed to have a rumpled, hurried look about them—making deadlines, no doubt. These are just boring memories.

One day, I was called to the visiting room to see a Mrs. Donald Honnen. When I entered the visiting area, she was standing with her back to me looking out the window. She was easy to recognize due to that tall, trim, professional, look about her. As I approached her, I extended my hand in introduction and said,

"Hi, my name is..."

She turned and looked directly at me for the first time, and in an emotional, quaking whisper, said,

"Oooh Bombeeee."

Now, that's the greatest memory of all.

BOUNDARIES

I've heard so many different reasons for why some of us act the way we do that, at best, I'm confused. To me, life is like a checkerboard with everyone owning a square. Some people build a nest in their square and live happy and care-free and with a known direction for their entire life. They don't question the boundaries. They are content with being told what is good and what is bad for them. They don't feel a need to experience things before they believe them.

Others—perhaps one in every 150—believe little of what they hear about life. Building their nest within the boundaries of their square bores them. They feel bridled in life. Their temporary comfort is within that square; and yet, they have a need to see what is outside.

However, when they venture out, they oftentimes do so in fear and they soon crave that fear. They can feel something is about to happen, are afraid it will happen, and yet they worry that it won't happen. A mixed bag of unsettling emotions that insure that this one-in-150, either crosses life's **BOUNDARIES** or tolerates life in sheer boredom.

JUST A TOUCH

I just finished reading a book about some Catholic nuns working in Calcutta with dying leprosy patients. *The House Of Death* is the name of the book. These caring and dedicated Sisters found they could comfort a dying patient just by touching them. Just a touch —the gentle, loving touch from someone who cares—God, how I know its importance.

I recall coming home after driving a log-truck all day, tired to the bone. It gets you right between the shoulders. After taking a long hot shower, I would lay down in the center of the living room, in the middle of the floor. I'd lie flat on my back, arms spread wide. My sons were little then—in pre-school. When they noticed me laying there, they stopped whatever they were doing. No healthy kid would pass up a chance to attack a grown person when he is flat on his back. I was in their world then. They could even look down at me for a change; I was their size. If they were a bit slow to react, I would just raise my head up, look directly at them and stick out my tongue. That's all it would take. Not only was I their size, and in their world, but I was lipping off too!

That can not be tolerated in their world, you know, so they would attack! I would hear high-pitched giggles, tinkling squeals, and even some outrageous grunts, as they attacked me. Oh, how I enjoyed the tinkle in their voices, seeing the sparkle in their eyes and joining in their laughter as I fought one hell of a battle.

7

I would also notice the tension leave my body. Memories of a bad day at work, even the tension between my shoulders, would be forgotten. I would grunt, laugh, and suffer the beating they gave me. After ten or fifteen minutes of that huffing and puffing, I sometimes said those magic words all little boys fight for—

"I give!"

That would get me out of some yet unnamed and fool-proof headlock only little boys know. Once they had won or lost, makes no difference, it was time to talk. Of course, I became something akin to a log at that point. They would either sit on me, or sit beside me and kinda lean on me. Then, if I was lucky, they would share some really good stuff with me.

"Ya know what Dad? Bill found a green snake and he gots it in a jar."

"Hey Dad, can you fix the wagon, 'cause the wheel fell off?"

"Dad, if we had a thousand-million-hundred dollars, would it cover up the whole house an' everything?"

The trick was to really listen—to really hear them. Then I would just relax and truly enjoy what took place inside me. Enjoy the touch of those little hands, share their little world, pay close attention to the simple questions they openly and honestly sought answers to. They let me live in their world for a few minutes. I could look up at those little faces as they asked questions to the smartest, biggest, toughest man they knew—me, their Dad. They would make my world simple, soft, close, and completely honest. Sometimes, if I was lucky, they would even share a secret or two with me. The bottom line was, the touch of those little hands. Sharing in their little world restored me, by disarming me of the anger and tension I brought home.

I wonder if that touch, and their simple honest world, isn't needed much more than we realize these days. I've laid in this prison cell so angry that my guts felt like they were vibrating over something that's not even worth mentioning today. I was angry and surrounded by everything hard and cold—concrete and steel.

We have programs in prison called, "Anger Management." I've taken them all and have even facilitated a few. They tell you all kinds of tricks: count to ten, beat on a pillow, and even hug a damn tree (that last one is called "getting grounded"). They've told me about *yin* and *yang*, in relation to the psyche, of inner response to outside stimuli, and even of subconscious responses. Most if it is a complicated line of pure speculation designed only to keep the damn fool who designed the program out of the unemployment line or nuthouse.

I'll tell you what calms most of the men I know. It's the touch, the unguarded love and understanding of a child; the tinkle in their voices, their trusting eyes, their laughter, and the natural closeness of them.

And, the gentle caring touch of a woman who smells of laundry soap or dish soap, not Chanel No.5. Yes, the woman who only has time to make you chicken noodle soup for dinner, because she has been cleaning and taking care of everything a man truly loves all day. That lady whose hair isn't perfectly made up, is maybe a little overweight, and has never owned a designer dress. That's what calms an angry man.

I can't count the tears I've shed, as I prayed for one more chance to wrestle with my little boys in the center of that living room floor; to share their simple world, hear the tinkle in their laughter, feel the touch of their little hands and to be called Daddy, just a couple more times.

I know nothing about leprosy or what those Catholic nuns must have experienced in Calcutta, but after countless nights in a prison cell, with only guilt as a companion, I do know what I miss most and what calms me. It's **JUST A TOUCH**, the gentle loving touch, of someone who cares.

FIGHTING THE WRONG
OPPONENT

Several times in the past I've felt that I was fighting some unseen opponent while boxing. Throw a punch and get three back, never seeing them coming. Fighting a good fast counter-puncher will make a person feel like he is surrounded at times. It's like seeing and knowing one opponent—the guy in front of you—and being hit by someone unseen.

When I came to prison in the early 1970's, I was scared to death. I knew all the horror stories; homosexual rapists, cold heartless killers, everyone carrying shanks (prison knives). Yes, I was scared. There was no way that I was going to let any of those animals I had heard and read about get me, not alive anyhow. As a matter of fact, I was pretty well resigned to the very real possibility that I would die in prison at the hands of one of those animals I had heard so much about.

Being 6-foot, 5-inches, 245 pounds, and in damn good physical shape (an accomplished boxer), I still worried about the surprise attack from some inhuman convict with a flat nose and an erection. I knew he was there somewhere within the prison walls. He had to be: I had seen him in the movies, on TV, read about him in books and newspapers, and had the cops (correctional officers) tell me in great detail of the depraved animals behind the walls.

I've had convicts point out famous criminals in the chow hall several times and was very surprised once to find out that a killer of several of his own family members was living in the next cell. But even *he* wasn't that monster that I knew was lurking somewhere inside the walls. As time went on, I relaxed—but always with my back to the wall, so to speak, always on guard. The men I knew best were scared like I was, even the killer of his family. The showers were always a source of tension with me—20 or 30 men packed into a steam filled shower room together. I kept my back to the wall and a damn good grip on the soap. Still nothing happened.

To date, I've never seen a homosexual rape in any Washington or Oregon prison system. I've heard they happen, but like the flat-nosed killer, still unseen. Although, I've met many media monsters, serial killers, robbers, rapists, and just about any criminal type known to man (in my search for these monsters who are known to be here behind these walls), what I found was a bunch of convicts, (uneducated for the most part), scared in some fashion, feeling ashamed, homesick and in shock, looking for some kind of answer as to what happened. Many had done something under the influence of some mind-altering chemical. Some had even committed crimes they couldn't remember and had passed lie detector tests to prove it. Alcoholic Black-out, they call it. Some others were mental cases, pure and simple. Anyway, for the most part, convicts feel more angry at themselves for what they have done than anyone else.

I've met a few men in prison that were totally innocent, such as Lucky Francis and Shannon Long. Both men are in the same prison system that holds the men who actually committed the crimes that Shannon and Lucky were sentenced for. In both cases, the real perpetrator of the crime stands ready to admit his guilt. He asks for a lie detector to prove it, but to no avail from the authorities. The Justice Department's own figures say two in ten are wrongly convicted—not innocent—wrongly convicted, and they seem satisfied to leave it at that.

On the other extreme, Northwesterners will not soon forget the names of Charles Rodman Campbell and Westley Allen Dodd. Both of these animals had killed kids. I have little doubt that, if either of them were given a work release job in any respectable logging community in the Northwest, somehow, somewhere, some member of that community, a Father or Grandpa, would have saved the taxpayers a lot of money that was given to attorneys for their appeal process.

Big, tough Campbell committed such vicious murders that hundreds of convicts, with violence in their records, were brought back from work release facilities and camps across the state. That could have been a problem for Campbell behind these walls, but he may have survived it. One of those victims, however, was an 8 year old girl, and the entire prison population knew what he had done. There are too many Fathers and Grandpas in here for him to have lived very long, and he knew it.

It would not be fair for me to continue painting a picture of the men behind these walls from the point of view of someone who has never seen how each of these men act under the influence of drugs or alcohol. I'm sure many of the men who now greet me daily—clear-minded, guilt ridden, and looking for answers—were monsters in their fog-minded intoxicated condition. I'm also sure there are men who greet me daily that will someday sit on death row, or worse—live for many years with the memory of their sins. So, I can't give a truly objective view of both sides of these convicts. I can tell only what I see and hear daily.

I do see the surprise registered on the faces of visitors who come into prison for Alcoholics Anonymous, Narcotics Anonymous, Toastmasters, Lifers' meetings and some school programs. It's a shock for them to see real humans in here. I can't blame them in the least, for I too, searched for that flat-nosed monster with the erection for years. I still see the monster on TV and read about him in the newspaper. If you will take the time to just visit one of these prisons as a guest, chances are that you will be surprised at the lack of monsters.

You see, it took years of walking with my back to the wall, with a firm grip on the soap, before I finally realized where, and who, the real monster was. It was the system itself. It tells the taxpayer to build more prisons. It gets millions of dollars while they tell the taxpayer these prisons are full of flat-nosed killers, rapists, and robbers when their own figures show that less than 50% of convicts behind these walls are such, and few have flat noses. They tell the taxpayers that they rehabilitate criminals but, over time, they brutalize inmates and create monsters, pure and simple (see *"The Making of Monsters"*).

I've often wondered how the public can allow a multi-million dollar tax drain off to a department that admits to an 77.7% overall failure rate over a 5 year period and calls itself a "Department of Corrections."

HARD

A person gets hard in captivity. Things seen and experienced have a way of taking the shock factor of violence away from us. We've seen worse, so many times, that it's not as shocking to us as it might be to someone lucky enough to have never experienced it.

I remember seeing the Rodney King beating on television for the first time. The younger inmates who were watching the TV were shocked. The older convicts thought it was bad, all right, but figured that King was lucky he had his clothes on.

Beatings with batons are not new to older convicts. They know a beating is a lot worse if a person is naked. Clothes give a kind of insulation between the baton and the skin. They also offer a padding to a person's joints, and a clothed person doesn't feel as helpless or exposed.

Naked is generally the way prison guards administer a beating to a prisoner. They wait until the prisoner is stripped naked, preparing to change into segregation coveralls before they attack. It's a common practice in the segregation units; if a prisoner had hit a guard, or was mouthy, or had done any of a number of things to really anger the segregation guards.

They would be stripped naked and beaten, exactly like Rodney King got it in the legs and below the neck, except that

King had his clothes on. If you remember, King's only visible mark was a black eye. Most of the blows he suffered were to the body. Take it from me, those body blows hurt. Those bastards know exactly what they're doing. Maybe that's why the older convicts didn't get excited over what they had seen of the King beating on television. They'd seen it and felt it many times before.

It might surprise some to know that most of the screaming going on during one of those beatings comes from the guards; the prisoner just whimpers and grunts.

It isn't that older convicts want to seem hard when they see a person on the television news shaken, while telling a story about being threatened with a weapon, assaulted, or robbed during a violent situation. Luckily, it happens fast on the streets. In prison, it's often more violent and lasts much longer.

For years, in every prison I've been in, it's been common practice for guards to transfer prisoners they dislike into cells with prisoners who are assaultive. For instance, if a guard dislikes a prisoner and knows the prisoner snores, he transfers the prisoner into a cell with a man who is assaultive and hates people who snore. The prisoner has two choices, move into the cell or get thrown into the hole and have his prison sentence extended due to loss of good time for refusing the guard's direct order to move into the cell.

There are many opposing likes and dislikes guards can use to get prisoners to attack each other. Put a sex offender in with a radical, a skinhead in with an African, a young lover of Rock music in with a older hard con who likes quiet Country music, and sooner or later there will be trouble. Prisoner-to-prisoner assaults, even though orchestrated by a guard, are always blamed on the prisoners. For the guards, it's a no-lose situation.

Unlike free people who are seldom exposed to their assailant for more than a few seconds, prisoners are often locked in a 6x9 foot cell with a person that assaults them, for hours, days, and even years. They are often forced to spend the night three feet from the very person that just beat and robbed them—behind a locked door. It's called double-bunking (two or more prisoners in a cell).

Most of the time double-bunking works okay, but it's also used to punish prisoners. I don't know a convict who has been in prison for over ten years, who hasn't experienced a situation set up by a guard. I've been beaten as badly as Rodney King several times over the years, and have been forced to transfer into a cell with a person that both the guard and I knew would create an immediate violent situation.

When older prisoners see someone on television complaining about facing a dangerous assailant for a few minutes, it's like falling in the shallow end of the pool to us. Victims of violence have every right to be scared and they should be. We've been caged with violence so many times, that we do understand your fear. Violence no longer shocks us, we've been living with it too long. We honestly never wanted to, nor realized, we were becoming this **HARD**.

CONVICT

I got a can of Top cigarette tobacco, a yellow 6oz can, on the shelf in my cell. It's damn near empty now. It comes with 200 gummed rolling papers. I roll my cigarettes by hand, and can do it one handed, if I have to. It's a lost art these days, rolling smokes by hand. I used to smoke Viceroys and Camels before I came to prison. I can't afford them in the joint. I'm so used to these harsh hand-rolls, Camels probably wouldn't satisfy me.

Doing time these days is almost a lost art too. Not many convicts left in prisons these days. There's a big difference between convicts and inmates, you know. Inmates have no respect for themselves or anyone else. Used to be if a convict kept himself, his language, and his cell, neat and clean, and did his own time(minded his own business); we said he had class. It was a description a man worked hard to get.

Today, the term isn't heard or understood. Personal hygiene has been downgraded to deodorant and colorful clothes. Cell odors are covered with deodorizers and incense, and a filthy mouth is called cool. Filth breeds filth, I guess. If a man is filthy in one area, he is filthy in them all.

Even prison violence has changed. Some years ago, if a convict had a problem with another inmate or some guard, he took it directly to that person and straightened it out face to face, with fists, if necessary. We used to call it, "Takin' it from the shoulder." You were judged to have courage or heart by doing things in that manner.

Today's inmate doesn't have the courage to fight his battles alone. He gets all his filthy, colorful friends, to back his play, to fight for him. Seems like they're either trying to make friends with a guard, thinking they're a guard; or they throw feces mixed with urine in the guard's face from behind locked and barred doors, instead of takin' it from the shoulder with the bastard. A cowardly act by any standard... Respectless.

It's not surprising that you seldom see inmates act like convicts these days. Some of them think they're cops, some feel they're better than everyone else, and some look like Sears & Roebuck catalog models. The old "Goon Squads" have been replaced with what's called "Decontamination Crews," (that clean up the feces). Snitching is called "gettin' down" and cell blocks smell like whore houses. Daily, I see inmates carrying on conversations with guards, laughing, having a good time with a sadist in uniform that no self-respecting convict would allow in his living room. Another weak, respectless deed.

I don't like, nor trust, the cute, sweet smelling, snitching, little heathens. They've sold out to an easy, disrespectful, self-serving way of doing time. They've become powerless in their failure to recognize a bond, a way of life, a togetherness, for who and what a man is. Sometimes these inmates make me glad that I'm a beat-up old **CONVICT**—with class.

ALL WE HAVE LEFT

The media says the crime rate dropped last year. Good news, they say. They claim to have come up with the right answers to curb crime. Well, they may have convinced you, but I know different, so let me explain. Let's look at what really happens in prison today, why it fails, and who creates failure on both sides of the bars.

When a person arrives at the Induction Center or Receiving Unit, on his or her way to prison, they remove everything dear to you. You keep nothing to remind you of a prior day when the amount of cash in your wallet was the only barometer of what you could possess. This happens to all people sent to prison; killers, rapists, and those who deliberately overdraw on their checking accounts.

Your clothes are the first to go. You are given the choice of sending them home or donating them to some charity. They probably won't fit when you get out anyhow. Same goes for your watch, shoes or boots, and any other jewelry with the exception of your wedding ring, if it isn't worth more than three hundred dollars, that is.

Then they take what is left of your pride and ability to make a common sense decision, with a command to bend over and spread your butt cheeks for a body cavity search. After this it's just a short step to getting you to eat, sleep, shower, see your loved ones, go inside, go outside, go to Church, go to school, get your mail, play sports, watch TV, and even get sick, only when and where they tell you to do it.

At that point, possibly your very first night in prison, you are forced to take inventory of what remains of the former you. Some give up and concede there is nothing left. This hits those who have been relatively sheltered in life hardest, those not brought up in a ghetto or housing project and have had known at least some family support in life. Even your name is changed to a number.

Some can be heard crying in the cool damp, darkness of that concrete and steel cell, on that hard bunk, with that coarse wool blanket covering their head, in a vain attempt to block out what the eye sees and the heart feels. Some find their answer only in suicide, some in mind-altering drugs, and some in different forms of anger.

This anger can come from behind an angry, hostile face; open and straight-forward violence, directed at the establishment and all that it represents. This is the road often chosen by the inexperienced; those who are shocked by the reality of how uncaring things truly are in America today.

Their long standing beliefs in fairness and justice have been destroyed. The fact is, that America incarcerates more people per capita than any other country in the entire world; more black men than South Africa incarcerated during the height of Apartheid. And, it is the only Nation that will execute a child.

The experienced, older convict releases anger behind a smiling face, a kind, disarming demeanor, and a submissive nature. He is not surprised by the injustice; he is convinced that the biggest criminals in this country do in fact run the Nation. He knows rehabilitation is a word used only by politicians to con taxpayers, and prison is only a College that offers a degree in crime.

In fact, longer prison sentences only extend the learning period for an angry mind. Experience has taught him to cost, in any manner, the establishment's most needed possession—money. This is nothing new really. The oppressed, or the underground, have fought their oppressors in the same manner for centuries.

It's war, plain and simple, declared by the Department of Justice, on the poor and underprivileged class, under the guise of justice. Anger of this type can be expressed by the deliberate destruction of state furnished products, such as food and clothing, to filing lawsuits over nothing, and the sabotage of expensive state material and equipment. Of course, this takes only a minor amount of organization and communication.

Now, we come back to the one single thing they can't take away from us when we get to prison....Our word.

Erosion of the pride felt in a person's word gets more evident each year. Today it's not unusual to see an inmate attempting to make friends with the establishment, turning their backs on their peers; as a matter of fact, working against the very people they are locked up with. This is done by informing, collaborating, and taking what their weakness deems the easiest way out.

They form small groups, teaching and talking violence, having others do their dirty work, while they themselves talk loudest and prey on the weakest. This also is not new, as collaborating with the enemy was done even in Biblical times.

They think only of themselves. Their psychopathic personalities are evident even in the antisocial world they share with other criminals. They are outsiders, who are not accepted in the free world. They are disrespected and shunned, even in prison. They weaken all those in whose company they are allowed to share. Truly, the Judases of today's world.

They are easily visible to those around them, due to their superior attitude, bullying mentality, and their constant bragging of violent deeds. It's an effort to cover the cowardice they feel. These cowards teach and live only to convince others, or possibly convince themselves, that their weak, spineless, intimidating ways are right.

In the world of prisoners they are called punks, snitches, wanna-be tough guys, or weak cowards. In society's world they are called Politicians. They care for no one but themselves. Known as liars, cheats, and self-centered egotists, who have a quick answer or excuse for everything. Their beliefs are easily bought and sold. However, with their cowardice and lies, they grow more open and obvious daily, in both worlds.

A generation ago, convicts were judged on their word, first and foremost. Convicts paid their debts in full, and on time; carried out their promises in full, on time; and threatened others only as a last resort, with the intent to carry out that threat, in full, on time. Loyalty was given in full, every time, without question, to all of one's peers.

It's important to recognize that the vast majority of people in prison have experienced abuse, poverty, discrimination, and therefore are not to be judged as normal. The few that enter any prison system relatively normal, will not leave as such.

Surviving in a hate-filled, subhuman environment, takes its toll on all that do time. Those of us who have done a lot of time will react faster to potentially violent situations, will give and demand complete loyalty from our friends, and will guard our innermost feelings and secrets much closer than what is deemed normal in society.

The uncaring, dictatorship-type of living has taught us that it's very dangerous not to do so. Protect yourself and those around you at all costs. The "us against them" mentality adopted by law enforcement, also holds true to experienced convicts.

The victim of this entire secret and often times deadly dance of crime, cop and criminal is, of course, society. They ask only that they be free of crime in their neighborhoods and they have that right. After all taxpayers pay millions of dollars every year for that failed goal. They never realize that the system taxpayers paid 849 million dollars into (the last Washington State budget), is the single biggest cause of the very violent crime they are paying to stop. A prison industry has been created in America, a taxpayer-funded monster that creates the violent criminal it's paid to eliminate.

This charge is not made without a basis of fact. Washington and Oregon have a 77.7% overall recidivism* rate over a five year period. The death rows of these two states house a total of 44 men, of which 41 are prison educated, ex-convicts (1998 statistics).

The term "Progressive Criminal Behavioral Pattern," used by this failed system is applied when a person increases the severity of the crime the person was originally convicted of. Believe me, "Progressive Criminal Behavioral Pattern," is nothing but the end result of a taxpayer-funded education in crime. Classes are taught daily in every prison in America, to every first-time offender. Recipes for crime are exchanged by criminals in a pressure cooker called prison where angry minds absorb every detail quickly. Longer sentences do little but give inmates more time to learn. It's so simple to those of us who have watched this monster grow over the years.

The exceptions are few, the failures many, and the crime rate spirals. The media tells the public crime rates are down, even gives statistics from National Agencies. Politicians who are quick to find answers, create laws making it all but impossible for the ex-convict to live anything close to a honest and normal life after release. This is done by sensationalizing the acts of a few violent Punks, and hiding the successes of the convicts who make a good honest effort at rehabilitating themselves.

I ask only that you check out the statistics I've quoted. Look out your window, pay attention to your local news, and then tell me that I'm wrong, that I'm a liar; that in fact crime really has dropped in the past year like the media says. Punks and Politicians, lying cowards, and that's **ALL WE HAVE LEFT!**

THINGS THAT TINKLE

Ever feel the relaxing sound of wind chimes? They seem to tinkle with an almost hypnotic gentleness. I've found so many gentle, tinkling things in my life that were once over-looked by me. The tinkle in my wife's voice when she said,

"Hi, how are you honey?" or, "How was your day?"

There's a tinkle there, a caring.

"Daddy, can I have a quarter?"

A tinkling child's voice.

There is something very calming about things that tin-kle. The squeal of a happy baby tinkles and makes the biggest and toughest grown men crawl on their knees barking like a dog. I've done it myself, had fun doing it too, and the reward-ing tinkle I received was priceless.

I don't honestly think there is a man alive big enough to make me do what a smiling, tinkling baby can. Ya know how you butt your head into the belly of a baby and let the baby giggle and pull your hair?

Remember how natural it feels, how much fun it is to be rewarded with giggles and tinkling squeals? That's pure, pristine, unguarded love, and it tinkles.

My wife's voice used to tinkle, I was just too stupid to hear it. I never gave a second thought about the bed I got out of every morning. I just got up and got ready for work, never even thought about my wife making that bed day after day. I took it for granted. The special dinners she made because I happened to like them were never truly appreciated by me.

Oh, I always said "thank you," and gave her a kiss, but never did I stop and think of all the work and time she put into making the many things she made for me. What amazes me today is how this woman could do all the things she did for me and still have the time to tell me in a tinkling voice that she loved me.

The tinkle doesn't work alone, however. Softness comes with the tinkle. My wife's soft hair against my cheek as she sleeps beside me. Her soft tiny hand in mine when we went shopping or just going for a walk and the softness, the rightness, I felt when she was in my arms. I remember not being able to get to sleep unless some part of my body was touching hers. My whole life was surrounded with soft things that tinkle. It's all just a memory now.

A man needs things that tinkle, things that are soft, yes, and love. I hear the laughter of a woman even here in prison from time to time, smell perfume too, on rare occasions. Now, it causes me to stop and remember, enjoy even, but at times it sparks regret, for the blind fool I've been. It sparks memories of the day when I didn't take the time to hear the tinkle and feel the softness that was all around me.

It's hard to imagine someone caring enough for me to make my bed these days, let alone clean up my mess or wash my coffee cups. I don't know if I can sleep in a soft bed with a comforter on it, instead of this hard steel bunk with a course wool blanket. Someone touching me in my sleep now days wouldn't do either of us any good.

Yes, there is something that calms me in the world of women and children. Something that is needed deep inside me. I need to talk babytalk and act like a damn fool seeking the reward of a tinkling baby's happy squeal; it calms me, it makes me whole. I'm not whole without soft hair against my cheek, without the softness of a kiss once in a while, or holding a tiny soft hand in mine. It all tinkles ... It's all softness... It's all love.

Guess this hard narrow steel bunk, surrounded by concrete and steel and the chill that goes with it, has made me appreciate softness and warmth. The constant roar of this cell block has taught me to value things that tinkle softly and the sheer loneliness of these walls has left little doubt of the desperate need a man has for love.

So, if you ever see a beat up old man smiling with pure enjoyment as he listens to children at play, women laughing, or chimes tinkling in the wind, with a tear in his eye... He is probably an old convict listening to **THINGS THAT TINKLE.** God knows, he's just trying to become whole again.

LOVE & RAGE

After reading some of my stories about love, it's only fair to write of the anger and rage I've known. I don't think it's possible to fully know any true feeling or deep emotion without first experiencing its opposite to the fullest. The powerful and gut wrenching feeling of rage can only be experienced during the absence of love. Anger left unresolved, turns to rage and rage, of course, is a direct path to insanity, death, or in some rare cases, survival. Walt Landor said,

"The flame of anger, bright and brief, sharpens the barb of love."

Perhaps this writing proves that statement in part. I find it hard to write of anger and rage these days. As a mental defense, while incarcerated, I've buried memories of such times under memories of love, need and softness. To write them is to relive those hate-filled moments, something not easy nor wanted by me today. I do it only to show the reader how amazingly powerful even the memories of love can truly be.

Also, writing about the beatings, stabbings and murders I've seen over the years,(at least the physical acts of them), would be redundant due to the many books and movies that have been made showing prison life from this shallow, uninformed viewpoint. Perhaps my telling as best I can the different emotions felt by me during some of these acts, would better serve the reader. With that in mind let me explain how rage, at least in my case, made me a survivor.

One of the many jobs I've held while in prison was that of a emergency room attendant in Washington State Penitentiary in Walla Walla, during the "Blood Alley" days of the early 1970's. My job was to take a gurney and go get the injured who couldn't make it to the hospital under their own power; to assist in any manner including suturing wounds, and at times spending the last hours with some dying young convict.

I received a letter one day addressed only to "Duke, C-17, 8 Wing." I remember wondering how a letter addressed only to my nickname could make it through the mail room censors. Whatever—I got the letter. It was from a young lady I had never heard of named Sheri.

Seems her boyfriend, a young inmate, had told her that some convicts were going to kill him and if she wrote me, I could stop it. I didn't recognize the name she gave me, but my cell partner, Leo Dobbs, did. Leo told me this boyfriend was no good, was a burn artist (didn't pay his bills), and was always in trouble.

"Don't get involved with that kind of thing, Duke," he told me, "the punk ain't worth it."

However, there was something in this young lady's words that wouldn't let me forget it, so I went to the people who were after her boyfriend. We talked and I took responsibility for the debt; the problem seemed taken care of. That done, I looked up the boyfriend. His name was Robbie Hanson, and I chewed his ass. First for scaring his girlfriend like he did, then for giving my name to a stranger, and then for not paying his bills on time. In the end he promised to never let it happen again and I believed him. What I didn't know was just how soon Robbie would break that promise.

Robbie was in the habit of leaving his drug debts unpaid until the last possible excuse he could come up with was exhausted. When all else failed he would offer a little gold ring with the word "LOVE" on it as collateral. This ring was his pride and joy, a gift from his girlfriend Sheri.

One day luck finally ran out. Tired of excuses, the man Robbie owed the money to came and claimed his Love ring. After thinking it over for a while, Robbie, in his ignorance, figured he was big enough to go and reclaim that damn Love ring. After all he was a weight lifter, an ex-high school football star and he knew damn well that he was a tough guy.

Well, they stabbed Robbie several times in the back with an ice pick. He mentioned it many times as he lay dying in front of me on the emergency room table, talking into my old cassette tape recorder, making one last tape for his Sheri. Between crying in disbelief and praying for forgiveness, he talked about how unfair it was for one man to stab him in the back while he was fighting with another. I've often wondered who in hell told Robbie that life in prison was fair.

For the last three hours of Robbie's life, I wiped piss off his face and chest with a damp cloth, while he cried in anger, spoke words into the tape recorder of love, and prayed for just one more chance. That happens, you know, when your kidneys are destroyed. You literally piss through your skin. The medical term for it is renal shutdown ... You don't even bleed.

Don't let this story about me standing beside a dying young inmate lead you to believe that I have always been a caring and gentle person. Far from it. Though as far as I know,

I've never taken a life. I have hurt many men with my fists, hurt some badly and even felt a type of rightness in doing it.

I spent countless hours looking at my reflection in a mirror; learning to smile in a friendly, relaxed and disarming manner and then bring a punch from belt height, in a split second, with either hand and break a man's jaw, never moving a single muscle in that friendly smile. I could smile at you and take the teeth right out of your head...with either hand. A jaw breaking sounds just like a pencil being snapped quickly. I've heard it many times.

I felt that most men killed in prison were men who didn't fight back very hard or were men the killer was sure he could handle. With that mind set, I wanted to make sure that if some punk ever got me, he would be easy to recognize. I started training to become a boxer. I, in my fear, elected to become feared, a fear generator, the true definition of a coward.

I loved boxing. It was a contest. There was a referee. I was young, strong and healthy. It occupied my mind, relaxed my body, it was fun. I lacked, however, the ability to turn off and on what is called the *killer instinct*. Fighting the average guy, exchanging blows, out pointing him in one on one competition; well, I just plain loved it. A fighter on the rebound from being knocked out in the sixth round by a heavyweight known as Claude "Hurricane" West, was looking to fight any local heavyweight at Marcus Whitman Coliseum in Walla Walla. He was called "The Rock." His real name was Rocky Reneker.

I was then a Minimum Security Inmate, housed outside the walls of Washington State Penitentiary, when I got permission to fight the Rock. As a matter of fact, several other minimum security inmates fought on the same card.

In the dressing room before the fight the Rock made a big mistake. He scared me. He called me a sleazy convict, a punk, a piece of scum, and got right in my face doing it. He also promised to hurt me real bad. He had me so scared that I was nodding my head in agreement with everything he was screaming in my face. The last thing he did before leaving that dressing room was to take the towel he had been wiping his arm pits and crotch with and throw it in my face, laughing as he left to get into the ring. I was so intimidated, so scared, that I just sat on the dressing room table and took it.

A friend who worked my corner that night would later tell me,

"I knew the Rock was beat when he threw that towel in your face, Duke."

Well, I sure wish old Leo had told me at that time because I was scared spitless.

Of the three men working my corner that night, (Leo Dobbs, Mike Spaulding and Jackie Moore), only Jackie is alive today. Leo was murdered in Yakima Washington, his killer yet uncaught. Mike Spaulding, brother to the Director Of Prisons, in Washington State, died of agent orange, and Jackie Moore, the ex Canadian Lightweight Champion, lives in the Tacoma area, the last I heard.

In that crowded Coliseum was about sixty fellow convicts from the Minimum Security Building (MSB), and in the third row was a lady I dearly loved, my wife Sheri. Yes, Robbie's girlfriend, the girl who sent me the letter. Besides fearing the Rock that night, I was afraid of being made to look bad by being knocked out in the first round, of making a fool of myself in front of everyone, even afraid that the woman in the third row, would see how scared I truly was.

The Rock started the fight off in style. With an over-hand left he cut the outer side of my right eye. I was so uptight that the muscles in my neck and shoulders wouldn't allow me to punch. All I could do was push, my punches had absolutely no velocity. At the end of round one, the Rock head-butted me causing a deep cut under my left eye. Bleeding, scared, and humiliated, I started the second round.

Something happened in the first moments of that second round, something I still can't explain. The Rock was hitting me with some pretty good shots, but he wasn't rocking me with his punches. He had thrown everything he had at me in that first round and hadn't even dazed me.

For some unknown reason that angered me. It made me so mad that the fear left and I started taunting him. The punk was all mouth, nothing more than a fear generator, a coward just like me. Before the second round was over, I saw the same fear in the Rock's eyes that he must have seen in mine in the dressing room.

Today I'm ashamed of what I did to the Rock in the remaining six rounds. I beat him so bad that my right hand is still deformed, broken in several places, from smashing Rock's face. I blew my nose on the face of my left glove and smeared it in his face. I spit down his back and in his face when he tried to tie me up in clinches. I used my elbows, palmed him on the off-referee side (the palm of a boxing glove has very little padding). Between the forth and fifth rounds, it was so bad my corner man Jackie Moore, slapped me several times screaming,

"Take him out, he is whipped for god's sake!"

I refused. The anger, the rage in me wanted to hurt him

more. The Rock had become the only thing in my world at that moment, just him and I and I wanted to hurt him bad. Jackie cut off my water after the fifth round and said he was ashamed of me. Those sixty fellow convicts could be heard over the rest of the crowd wildly screaming,

"Kill the head; the body will die! Get him Duke! Kill the punk!"

And I tried. Not to knock him out, no, to keep on hurting him. All my own stuffed anger, fear, and cowardice, had turned to rage. My broken hand didn't even hurt, I didn't hear Sheri screaming in the third row, there was no feeling of fairness nor of this being a sporting contest. No... Hell no ... It was pure rage.

After the fight in the same dressing room I took the towel I had been wiping the blood off my face with, rubbed it on my crotch and shoved it into the Rock's face. I called him all the names he had called me before the fight. He just sat there in fear and took it. The look in his eyes still bothers me to this day. Total defeat, the look of a proud man beaten to a pulp, in shock, on the verge of tears. He didn't even try to push that bloody towel away.

For years I was proud of that fight and I'm ashamed to say I even bragged about it. Today, if I could meet the Rock face to face again, it would be me on the verge of tears, asking him for forgiveness. The look on his face when I was rubbing that bloody towel in it has haunted me countless nights. I've often wondered who in the hell told the Rock that a scared convict, in fact a intimidated coward, would fight fair. After all, fairness is seldom even condoned in prison these days.

*NOTE, for you diehard fight fans. A fighter's gear consists of a belt/cup, trunks, and a pair of BVDs. The BVDs are not unlike a woman's panty girdle.

"Just in case you tear the rear end out of your trunks," they tell you.

Wrong! The truth is, when Emil Griffith beat Benny "The Kid" Parett to death on national television in Madison Square Garden, (due to a slow call by the referee), "The Kid" lost control of his bowels. It happens more often than you might think. A good solid knockout often results in the fighter losing control of his bowels. And, of course, boxer shit doesn't do much for Budweiser sales these days.

WEBSTER'S POCKET DICTIONARY says a coward is: One who shows shameful fear or timidity. Fear to many of us, especially those of us in prison, is a daily companion. In my sickness I lived with fear to such a degree that to not be alone with my fear, I projected fear to others. In fact, I enjoyed seeing fear in others, it made them like me. Thus in English-speaking America, by definition, I was a coward, because I admit to showing shameful fear and timidity. I also believe, that had I not let the words of another alter my focus from the sport I loved so much, I may well have lost that fight. The rage I allowed in myself made me a survivor in the ring.

At gut level, whenever I allowed myself to forget about two of my life's loves, boxing and the lady in the third row, it opened the door for rage. It is my belief that rage isn't possible whenever the memory of love is present. I've learned a lot from the women in my life.

In their unmanliness, they are much braver than most men. You see, I believe that if our roles had been reversed, had the lady in the third row been the fighter and had I been in the third row; she would have had the courage to come to me and say she was scared, that she didn't want to fight and maybe even cry a little. She saw the act of what I thought was so manly for what it truly is, shameful timidity, afraid to admit the fear one feels.

If you could ask Sheri today, she would tell you that my hands are warm, soft, and gentle. Rock Reneker will not agree. Sheri screamed her heart out that night. She begged me to promise her that I would never fight again. I didn't make her that promise and fought three more fights. She did, however, refuse to ever watch me fight again.

She was no softy, if you think that pretty little 100 pound lady wouldn't fight any 220 pound heavyweight in my defense, you are wrong. She has always been more than my equal. She could drink whiskey right out of the bottle—when she felt like it, she could go camping and rough it with the best—when she felt like it and she would call me "Her Big Old Lover Duck," if even when I don't want her to—when she felt like it.

Yet she could be the height of grace and femininity, someone I'll forever be damn proud of, when she felt like it. Perhaps, someday I'll have just half the courage Sheri had, the courage to go to someone I love and trust and say the unmanly thing,

"I don't want to do this—I'm scared," if I really am.

So, take it from this old coward; never forget the love you feel, because even your memories of **LOVE** will defeat **RAGE.** EVERY... SINGLE ... TIME.

HE HIT ME

One of my best friends in prison was Leo Dobbs.

Leo and I lived in the same small cell, C-17-8 wing at the Washington State Penitentiary for several years. Leo tried to make a boxer out of me. I never did make it, however. He finally told me,

"The trouble with you, Duke, is ya can't fight a nice guy." Guess that meant I didn't have that old "killer instinct."

One day, I was classified to be sent to the minimum-security building outside the walls. This meant that I would be leaving my best friend alone in the cell we had shared for years. Leo and I didn't talk about my leaving; we kept quiet, avoiding the subject. We didn't know what to say, anyhow.

When the day finally came, Leo helped me pack all my worldly possessions into three boxes. I left him my radio so he could have something to listen to. He gave me his best bag gloves and a couple pairs of socks he said he didn't want anymore.

With that done, Leo helped me carry my entire worldly possessions over to the prison release area. When I bent down to set the box I was carrying on the floor, Leo let go with an overhand right from hell. He hit me solidly in the chest, knocking me back into the wall and taking my breath away.

He then turned and walked away, quickly saying,

"Gotcha, asshole," as he left.

Grunting for air against the wall, I couldn't even talk. However, I did see Leo wipe a tear off his cheek as he turned to leave.

You see, this close friend, the man who saved my life, shared the pain of my divorce, fought with me against one and all, drank with me, and even used the toilet in front of me in our tiny cell, for years, had like me, lost his ability to openly say,

"Goodbye friend, I'm gonna miss you."

We did exactly what prison had taught us to—to strike out when confused or in pain, to never show honest emotion, and to never, ever cry, no matter what.

So if Leo hadn't hit me—we both would have cried... That's why I'm glad **HE HIT ME**.

FROM A CRYING MOTHER

Just got a letter from an old cellmate's mother. She writes the standard greetings, tells of her problems getting to work during a cold spell we just had, and a few complaints about the prices of things these days. Finally, near the end of the letter, she tells me of going to see her son in Washington State Penitentiary, (a few days prior to writing the letter). She tells me that he is okay, not "good okay," she stresses.

He seems different and she wonders if there is a possibility of him trying to kill himself. Then she tells me that two members of her family have committed suicide in the past and that if her son did the same thing, it would kill her.

This mother never had written me before. She knew very little about me other than that I was in the same cell with her son for a few months in the past. She had only one son, had never been exposed to the prison system before, and now she was confused and scared for him. She was asking for an answer to something that I could only guess at.

It was the same old story as far as her son went. He was angry at being reduced to a number, a security rating, and being treated as a subhuman. He was acting different because he was different. His mother saw these changes as depression, and she was right.

I could tell her that her son would be his old happy self again as soon as he settled down a bit within the system and got used to things, but I knew different. He would only get better at hiding his anger, masking his hate with a smile and even laughter. As far as his killing himself, that was anyone's guess. Most first timers don't, but it happens.

Since he had a family history of suicide, I'm sure the odds were not as good as they might have been. I knew too that if this mother told this same story to prison officials, by phone or letter; her son would be placed on suicide watch in the hole and a record of it would become a part of his permanent file for the remainder of his life. It would in fact follow him throughout the prison system forever. Then, there is the very real possibility of her son being placed on strong mind altering drugs, should prison officials become aware of her concern.

So, what do I tell this crying mother? Do I tell her to pray? Damn right, she better do that. Do I deepen her fear by telling her the truth? Do I tell her that her son is now inside a beast that knows only numbers and has grown so large in its importance, that it is out of control? No, I think not.

Do I tell her to talk to her minister or priest, to go through the official channels, thus allowing the beast even more control of her son? I can't tell her about my own experiences within the system and what I know will be happening to her son. How do I tell a crying mother that her only son, the little boy her heart and soul needs, the boy that has never been away from her for more than a few weeks at a time since he was born, is being turned into a very angry man that will have an 77.7% chance of returning to prison? No, I do what follows:

Dear _____

Thank you for a great letter. Sorry to hear about the frozen streets and ice in your area; you better be careful. So, you got to see Sonny at the walls. Kinda looks like an old castle or something, doesn't it?

I'm sorry to hear about your concerns in regards to Sonny. He is a good strong kid, both mentally and physically; you should be very proud of that fact. He is going through some very different and changing times right now, so he could be depressed at times. We all go through it when we first get to prison.

I've just finished a letter to him. I told him to get into school, to attend any and all meetings where he can meet people from the outside who come in as guest volunteers. I told him to get into sports, to watch TV a lot, instead of letting his mind run wild in his cell and I told him to attend church as much as he could. I also explained to Sonny, that the three biggest enemies he has right now are sheer boredom, social arrest and the anger that comes from being constantly degraded.

I also told him to give his mother a break, that she is doing time just like he is and feels even more helpless than he does. So, in closing, let me just say that I understand your feelings and the best advice I can offer is to write him often, even if it's only a card, send him $10.00 once in a while and let him know that he is still loved very much. That will give him the strength he needs so badly right now.

Respectfully,
Duke

Guess that makes me as bad as this beast for not hav-ing the heart to tell the truth to this crying mother. As bad as I hate it, I find myself protecting others from truly knowing the vicious uncontrolled monster prison has become, out of shame for what it really does to their loved ones. Hopefully, my own family will never know what I too have been forced to experience in prison. There are just too many **CRYING MOTHERS** out there already.

"THE DEUCE"

To the Texas prison inmates who survived it, it's called simply "The Deuce." To the media and families of those inmates, it's known as the "The Riots on the Ramsey One Unit, of the Texas Department Of Corrections (TDC)." To me, a survivor, it's remembered as one of the most violent events and biggest cover-ups I had ever witnessed.

Two riots in eleven days, both the direct result of a policy developed by the then-Director of the Texas Department of Corrections and George Beto, an ordained Lutheran Minister. The Beto System was instituted to save taxpayers money. It created jobs for inmates known as Building Tenders, Turn Keys, Special Porters, Count Boys, and Dog Boys.

These jobs, in fact, made key-carrying guards out of inmates. They carried guns, were issued knives, were able to write up other inmates and had control of much of the prison. Building Tenders regularly beat other inmates bloody and, in some cases, to death. Prisoners were beaten for oversleeping, talking in the chow hall, not cleaning their cells or talking to a Uniformed Officer without permission. These beatings were condoned and supervised by Uniformed Officers on a daily basis.

In 1980, inmate David Ruiz managed to get a hand-written legal "Writ" smuggled out of Ramsey One Unit to Federal Judge William Wayne Justice in Houston, Texas. Judge Justice ordered an immediate stop to the brutality and ordered his Federal Marshals to enforce this ruling. Texas Corrections Officials chose to disregard these orders, and to stall as long as possible.

As tension mounted inside the prison, Building Tenders elected to use a heavier hand in forcing the prisoners to work. Beatings were common place, an almost hourly occurrence. August 19th, after returning from the fields about thirty prisoners attacked and killed four Building Tenders in the shower area. As a result, the Ramsey One Unit was placed on lock down.

Building Tenders stood back and watched as special Riot Squads of Uniformed Officers, in lock step and in full riot gear, went cell to cell assaulting prisoners. This assault went on constantly for forty hours, day and night, cell to cell. What little personal property prisoners had was destroyed, family pictures torn up, toiletries dumped out, stamps and writing supplies thrown away. Prisoners were stripped naked, their cells stripped of everything, and beaten with night sticks as we walked through a gauntlet of Uniformed Officers, to and from our cells. August 23rd, the beaten prisoners were forced to return to the fields.

Now, however, Uniformed Corrections Officers replaced the Building Tenders, as ordered by Judge Justice. The taunting of inmates by Officers and Building Tenders was in high gear. The Officers took every opportunity to exert their power over the prisoners by threatening, screaming, assaulting, and harassing them, for what "they" called a riot, (the killing of the four Building Tenders).

August 29th, after six days of this bullying, at about , 5:20, AM, those Uniformed Officers and their Building Tenders, found out what a real riot was all about.

I was exiting the chow hall after the breakfast meal and noticed about twenty Uniformed Officers standing in the hall near the Control Center. They were laughing and talking about, "This Ole Thang, and that Ole Thang," (a slang term used to degrade prisoners). The Major and the Captain, the two highest ranking Uniformed Officers, were laughing and enjoying their little get together.

The Major was the highest ranking Uniformed Officer on the Ramsey, a big man, 6'6", maybe 300 lbs. He had red hair and was called Red Rider, by the prisoners. I always figured that the Major was a weak, spineless coward, due to his aggressive and sadistic nature.

The captain, was a small man, 5'10", and maybe 150 lbs. He was known to be a smart-mouthed, vicious little bastard by most of the prisoners. One of the Officers standing with them taunting and laughing was the Dog Sgt. The Sgt. called a prisoner over to the group of Officers and said,

"Old Thang, are ya gonna give me a good days work or am I gonna have to beat your old ass again today?, " to the amusement of the Uniformed Officers.

The inmate, Ben Ulmer, started screaming as he charged into the twenty Uniformed Officers, screaming and swinging.

The Sgt. was the first to go down. Ulmer hit him square in the face and started after another Officer. For a few seconds the Officers stood frozen in shock. When it dawned on them what was happening, they seemed to concentrate on getting control of inmate Ulmer, paying no attention to the build up of prisoners in the hallway.

Before they knew what was happening, about a hundred prisoners rushed down the hall, out of the chow hall directly into the group of Officers. The captain started screaming at the prisoners to get back to their cell blocks when he was hit directly in the face, knocking him down. The other Officers grabbed their mace cans and started spraying the prisoners with gas in effort to gain control.

The Major turned and tried to get out an open electric gate about fifty feet away; I remember seeing him go down twice and regain his footing. The captain, disappeared under a fighting mass of prisoners, Officers, and mace. When the Major got to the gate, he was naked except for his police belt and one cowboy boot—he had literally fought right out of his clothes ... And the gate was closed. He just dropped to his knees and started crying.

Some prisoners took the Major's handcuffs out of his police belt and put them on him. With his hands cuffed behind his back, a prison issue belt was placed around—his neck and he was led out of the hall, much like one would lead a horse. The captain, was curled up in a fetal position on the floor, being kicked by several prisoners. The remaining Uniformed Officers were either down being beaten or already cuffed with their own handcuffs.

The smell of mace was so heavy it was hard to breath. Prisoners were spraying mace into open wounds, while others sprayed mace into guards' mouths, eyes, and openly hitting and kicking them. There was a lot of screaming those first few minutes of the second (real) riot. The Officers not caught in the Control Hallway ran for the side gate and were let out of the compound by the Tower Guard who controlled it. Steam hoses used for cleaning the kitchen were extended out into the hallway and pushed through the gas ports in the Control Center. It took only about ten minutes and the Officers in the small Control Booth were forced to open the doors to breathe.

The waist chains and leg irons kept in the Control Center were quickly used to chain up all the hostages. Once all the Officers were naked and chained, groups of prisoners spread out around the compound to look for more Officers that may be hiding out. None were ever found, but the speed in which the Uniformed Officers escaped, deserted their comrades, was the source of much laughter among the prisoners. The lazy bastards can really run when their asses are on the line.

I returned to the chow hall to search for some canned food and something that could be used to hold water. From prior experience, I knew they would shut off all water and power to the prison as soon as the back up squad got there. I found two cases of canned peaches, a big water cooler jug, and started back to my cell. In the ten minutes it took me to get those items the screaming had settled down. The captain was hanging by leg irons naked and upsidedown from the bars in front of 4 Wing. He seemed to be unconscious, his left arm obviously broken and his face beaten to a pulp. Several of the other Uniformed Officers were laying face down naked and bloody, in the dayroom in front of 5 and 6 wings. There was a lot of blood around and the mace was still almost fog-like in the air.

When I got to the second tier of 3 Wing on my way back to my cell, I passed the Major, bent over, hands cuffed behind his back, and tied by the belt around his neck to the second tier railing. He was blind because his eyes had swelled shut and was whimpering something about having grand children. He still had only one cowboy boot on.

Most of the prisoners were running around trying to find weapons, getting canned food and some were covering the windows so, when reinforcements arrived, they wouldn't be able to see inside the cell blocks. Several inmates had put on guards uniforms and some were screaming about killing all the guards. Most however, were preparing for what we all knew was coming, a hell of a battle when the reinforcements arrived. I spent some time getting the water container filled, hiding the canned peaches as best I could, and then walked back to the kitchen area to see if there was anything left we could use in the cell.

When I got to the Control Area, several inmates were shoving balls of paper down the captain's throat with a broken broom handle. He had blood coming out of his mouth and nose, but was conscious. What was left of the broken broom was sticking out of his ass. I found out later that these inmates had found a bunch of paperwork in the Captain's Office and were making him eat it. I've heard that the captain lived and also that he died later, I don't know what is fact because I didn't see him for the next three days.

The Major was led around like a horse, tied bent over, to the railings or bars with the belt around his neck, sodomized and beaten, regularly for the remaining three days. I know that he lived because I saw him several months later when his daughter brought him back to the Ramsey One, as part of his mental therapy.

The Major looked right at me and started crying, saying,

"Thank you, Yankee, for helping me."

What I did, was do nothing to him. I didn't hit him, didn't sodomize him or hurt him in any way. I didn't help him a bit, but because I didn't hurt him, in his mind, he felt that I was a help of some type. Out of the remaining hostages, all but four Officers who were respected for their fairness were beaten badly. Those four were kept locked in a cell, fed, given water, and were under the guard of prisoners, to insure their safety.

A small group of prisoners had the Dog Sgt, who's face was covered with feces, begging for his life. They had set up a Kangaroo Court designed to be like the one that he had, in the Sergeant's office, when he was Disciplinary Hearings Officer. The prisoners sanctioned the Sergeant by giving him the choice of eating feces, being sodomized, or being beaten with a police night stick. The Kangaroo Court was in session for the first two days with all but four Uniformed Officers, being sanctioned for some past deed.

The first night, the prisoners started looking for Building Tenders. They had about fifty of them in the first two cells in 3 Wing, the rest were in hiding around the compound. The Building Tenders suffered more than anyone with the exception of the Major, the Captain, and the Dog Sgt. The Building Tenders readily told which Officers had ordered them to do different things to different prisoners. The Officers were also pointing fingers at the Building Tenders. They all claimed to be innocent, of course.

Trying to sleep was almost impossible. The stink of Mace was everywhere (it's amazing how long that stuff lingers) Prisoners were looting the Infirmary Commissary. Many were high on the drugs taken from the infirmary. Some were trying to convince the others to give up, some wanted to kill all the hostages and some wanted to try a mass escape.

It was finally agreed that the hostages and Building Tenders, should be held in the kitchen vegetable room. It was big enough to hold them all near several propane tanks. There they would be close enough to those tanks, so, if needed, the valve could be opened and lit with fire, so that all the hostages would burn to death.

Outside the prison the entire perimeter was lined with off-duty Officers, State Police, and even some farmers from the area, all heavily armed. The Warden was talking over a bullhorn, asking for a meeting or some type of communication in an effort to bring this thing to an end.

For the next two days the Warden tried to arrange some kind of parley. He was told that it was too late to talk, he had been warned many times over the past year and didn't want to talk then, now' they felt it was too late, and that he could go to hell. The Warden was told about the propane tanks and how the hostages would fry before he could get through the first gate coming in. The prisoners did offer to trade six of the captured Uniformed Officers for the Warden...but he refused.

Finally on the third day, Federal Marshals and the National Guard arrived. An Army Captain and several Federal Marshals came into the compound. The Marshals brought us a signed order from Federal Judge William Wayne Justice. The order stated that TDC would be fully investigated by Federal Officials, and the violence and human rights violations would be stopped immediately, no more inmate Building Tenders, no more rule by George Beto's, "Building Tender System." The Federal Marshals then ordered us to return to our assigned cells so they could bring order back to the Ramsey. We did exactly as ordered, thus the fight with reinforcements we had expected was avoided.

The Major and the Dog Sgt. retired, physically beaten and mentally broken. I don't know what happened to the Captain, what ever it was, the vicious little son-of-a-bitch earned it. Several Uniformed Officers and Building Tenders— Curtis Brooks, Willie Barry, and Corpus Powell, were hospitalized with broken bones suffered after being thrown off the second tier in 3 wing countless times. As far as I know, none of the Uniformed Officers, who found out what a real riot was, ever returned to the Ramsey One.

*I learned a lot from that riot. I found that regardless of a man's station in life, be it cop or con, the men who growl the most, speak the loudest and make the most threats, will break the easiest when blood and teeth start flying. I learned that only so much can be taken from a man before he finds death preferable to how he is living. When humans are abused mentally or physically, past a given point, their life becomes less valuable to them. Fear of death and or self survival becomes only a distant memory. As a matter of fact, we were so beaten mentally and physically, that trading our lives for theirs seemed like a damn good deal to us. Death can become, in cases like that of George Beto's Building Tender System, preferable to life ... At its worst.

**The only record of the riot is in Law Books, "Ruiz v. Estelle, 679 F.2d III5, II54 (5th Cir.) I982." If anyone doubts what I have written here, please research the aforementioned case. Keep in mind that the Texas Department Of Corrections covered up all but some bare facts in the Court Records. To this day, the Beto System is deemed to be a successful policy in the Annals of Corrections. I can agree with that assessment in part.

The Director of Corrections was fired, several Wardens were fired or imprisoned and the Federal Investigation brought up criminal charges against several upper level Officials resulting in their going to prison themselves. To me that's success, making all those bastards suffer.

The only physical part I played in the riot was to tighten every handcuff on all but four (the same four that weren't beaten by the other prisoners), of those Uniformed Officers as tight as I could, every chance I got; repayment for the times they had done it to me.

I know a Major, Captain, Sergeant and many Building Tenders, who may disagree with the successfulness of the Beto System however.. I found out too, that I was right about the Major being a spineless bastard, but to this day my most vivid memory of the riot is that of the Major.

As bad as I hated that sadistic, red-headed bastard, I felt sorry for the naked, beaten, crying man, being led around like a horse, limping, because he had only one cowboy boot on. I've often wondered if the Texas Officials had any idea how close those hostages came to being cooked alive, or if they even cared.

It seems to often be the case, some high paid official make a rule or policy; then the people who have to live by that policy too often die for it. In that respect, the Major and the Uniformed Officers were as victimized by the violence generated from the Beto System as the prisoners were. If the sole barometer used to define the success of the Beto System was saving tax dollars, it was a success. The destruction of, and to, life must be overlooked, if that is the case. The damage done to both Uniformed Officers and prisoners can never be calculated ... We all suffered...We all lost.

*** Have you ever been on the edge of a high diving board unsure if you wanted to jump or not? Remember those few seconds of indecision? That's how close those hostages came to death during **The Deuce**.

MY WARNING

Beauty can come after hell, at least here on earth. Yes, the most beautiful, fulfilling, loving feeling I've ever experienced came after one of the most hate-filled violent moments of my life.

For several years after the death of my son Kent, I regularly challenged God in prayer. I begged God to show himself, to just let me have one look at his cowardly being, to give me one chance to break his jaw, beat him like he had beaten me, even kill him like he let a farm tractor kill my son. I begged and pleaded on my knees in prayer for a chance to attack God.

The anger and guilt I carried, coupled with my size, 6'5 and 260 pounds, made me a very dangerous and unpredictable man. I fit right in at the Southern Penitentiary where I was sent. It was designed for men just like me, men who had lost themselves, lost any reason to be nice, given up on life and the pain it continuously offered.

I fought constantly over anything. I looked for reasons to fight. The other convicts called me *Yankee* and did their best to stay away from me. The pain of a cut and beaten body was a welcome relief over the constant mental pain I knew so well.

My days were spent working in the river bottoms and swamps, chopping and picking cotton, okra, and cane. We worked with what is commonly known as a garden hoe. However, the tool we used was much heavier and was called an "aggie."

In the summer, the heat seemed to radiate back up off the dry ground. Men dropped from heat exhaustion hourly. The snakes were everywhere, mosquitoes and leeches constant companions. The prison guards rode horses and were addressed as "Boss." We were regularly beaten with clubs, horse whips and a long thin cane pole called a "thumper." Each night, when I got in after working 14 or 16 hours with that "aggie," I was dog tired. But, seldom so tired that I forgot to call God every name I could think of, in prayer, before I went to sleep.

There was one horse-mounted prison guard who seemed to go out of his way to give me a hard time. He found out that I had a fear of snakes and often took it upon himself to throw live snakes on me when I least expected it.

One day, I decided that enough was enough. In my sick hate-filled mind, there was only one way to take care of the problem; I was going to kill the guard. It was no monumental decision; it was nothing more than buying a pack of cigarettes. I would kill the bastard and what happened after that was of no consequence to me, no more than killing one of the many snakes he threw on me.

The morning was cool, the day I was going to kill that guard. It was early, about 8:00 a.m. My plan was to let him get close behind me on his horse and swing around quickly with my aggie and hit him in the face with it as hard as I could. I had a good heavy aggie with a six foot handle, so he would be easy to reach. I told the man working next to me to duck when I coughed, so he wouldn't get in my way.

The guard did exactly as I knew he would. He rode up close behind me and started talking.

"Da ya'll think I ken get this here ole yankee ta jump around a bit taday if'n I ken find me one o' those little ole tiny snakes?," he asked, as if talking to the other inmates.

I coughed and swung my aggie as hard as I could. The guard's horse spooked and threw his head up, deflecting the aggie upwards. The aggie came close enough to the guard's face to knock his hat off. His horse started acting up and he was trying to draw his gun and control the horse at the same time. I charged him as he fired.

The bullets spun me in a complete circle, never knocking me off my feet. The first shot hit me on the left side of my head and exited my mouth, the second shot hit my left arm pit and lodged in my lung, the remaining three shots hit the cheek of my butt and two times in my right leg. I felt none of them, only tasted blood and grit in my mouth. The guard, his horse, and I were all down in a kicking screaming pile of blood, rage, sweat, gunsmoke and fear. I remember grabbing the guard's now empty gun and hitting him with it and the horse kicking and screaming, before I passed out.

Can you imagine what cool fresh lilacs would smell like if you could totally fill your lungs with such pleasant pure freshness? Then imagine what total, complete love and understanding, would be like in a pain free, weightless, atmosphere, that had a safe rightness about it, like being welcomed home by someone you dearly loved, after a long and pain-filled journey.

Well, that's not half of the wondrous feeling I experienced. I'm not capable of putting into words the feeling I had. I didn't see a light at the end of a tunnel. I didn't feel as if I was traveling or in a void of any type. I was standing upright, feeling better than I ever imagined possible, looking at a being in front and above me, who was smiling at me and just radiating complete love and understanding.

This being had his arms spread wide and down, palms towards me. Slowly, with love and complete understanding, the being's arms raised, palms still towards me, as if to say, " Slow down, everything will be okay."

When that happened—at that exact moment—I knew without a doubt that everything would be okay. There was no doubt whatsoever in my mind. It was pure communication— complete understanding. It was un-questioned.

The other thing I remember vividly is everything was pastel blue, pure white, silver and gold. I recall a beautiful smell and music like tinkling crystal, yet it was softly quiet and totally free and pure.

I woke up in Ben Taub Hospital in Galveston Texas and was later transferred to John Seely Hospital in Houston. I'm not sure if I have those hospitals in the right cities, it may be vice versa. However, the records will have it right. When I came to, a nurse told me my heart had stopped three times. I had in fact died.

What I experienced was not like any near death experience I've ever heard about. I personally don't give a darn if you believe this writing or not and I invite your investigation of the physical anatomy of this story

I looked into the face of what I believe was Jesus, and there ain't a man on this planet big enough to make me believe otherwise.

Another thing, if you're an atheist, I'm not real good at turning the other cheek yet, so if you don't believe this, don't try to feed me some intellectual speculation about hallucinations; you may not get a good Christian response.

I know EXACTLY what I saw and: **BEAUTY CAN COME AFTER HELL.** So there!!!

WEEKS

What used to be years is now a matter of weeks; the reality of being released from prison is setting in. The feeling is like going in for a long-awaited and serious surgery. It offers a better life, more freedom from pain, but is fearful in its 'must be done' nature. The fear is of the unknown, re-entry into a society that has been in constant change for the past thirty years.

Do I even possess the flexibility of mind to absorb all these changes? Am I now too old to ever be comfortable enough to sleep behind an unlocked door? If so, will my social retardation and discomfort eventually force me to live as a hobo, eating in soup lines, my bed a sleeping bag, constantly a stranger, running from what has become a very real alien world to me?

Over the years I've learned to live progressively deeper within myself, constantly guarding against exposing the real me. Perhaps 10% of my thought process is exposed in conversation. The remainder, the real intellect, the emotion, the pride and feelings—90% of the former me—was long ago buried out of necessity and is often deliberately suppressed by me today.

I've got to rediscover who I am, in a world I know little of, or return to being 10% of who I was—in a cage. I've learned to sleep in comfortably, and settle for being a fraction of who I am.

However, on a positive note, my cell partner, a notorious snitch, the tattle-tail of my mentality, feelings and emotions—my typewriter—exposes a little of the former me, part of the hidden 90%, from time to time. Thus I'm less of a stranger to those who read my writings.

I'll no doubt forever reject anyone's pity or sympathy. But in shame and honestly, I'll admit my fear, confess to being less than whole, and I'll pray for society's understanding.

Yes, the years have become **WEEKS.**

ADDICTION

I want to tell you about a few battles I've fought in prison with some tough opponents in the past. My hope is that, like in the fight game, you will better understand what this truly dangerous opponent is. All the opponents I've fought have a specialty of some type.

Blackie Palmer, a convicted killer, was good with a knife. He had fast hands, carried his knife waist high, centered, openhanded enough to transfer it to his other hand in a split second. Blackie always came straight at you too. He was small, maybe 5'8, 175 pounds, and was known for the killing he did with his knife.

Blackie and I had a disagreement over a friend. He called me out to fight in the old RGC (Resident Government Counsel) Office at Walla Walla. This was done in front of several other men, so I didn't have the option of backing away. Besides, I was a good counter puncher and I felt I could take him.

The problem was, he had a knife and was good with it. I knew a knife would only retard my hand speed, so I didn't bring one. The RGC Office was under what is now the WSP Library. When I entered the office there was about 20 men waiting to watch the fight, several friends of mine and his friend.

Talk wasn't in vogue in those days, so as soon as the door was shut, Blackie came directly at me. He had his knife centered and transferred hands about three feet from me. When he brought his left hand up, I attempted to slap the knife out of his hand. I missed and he transferred hands.

A split second later he buried the knife in the left side of my chest. I felt it grate on my ribs. The fingers on my left hand went numb instantly and my mouth started filling with blood. As Blackie held on to the knife; a reflex caused me to clamp my arm down immediately, trapping his hand and the knife under my left arm. With my free hand, I hooked Blackie several times to the head, knocking him cold. When he went down, he pulled the knife out and down with him. About two minutes later, I also passed out.

Blackie and I spent about three weeks in the hospital; me with a punctured lung and him with several fractured facial bones. I fought Blackie one more time. Neither of us won. However, I didn't require hospitalization after the second fight and he did.

Over the years I've fought many tough men with my fists on prison yards of Oregon State Pen, Leavenworth, Kansas and Walla Walla. I crawled into the boxing ring with tough men eleven times. Two of those men were ranked heavyweights; "The Rock," who I beat and wrote about in "*Love and Rage*," and a heavyweight out of Seattle, ranked tenth in the world at the time I fought him.

That heavyweight from Seattle beat me like he owned me. To this day, I have scar tissue behind my left eye that bothers me as a result of that fight. He broke both my upper and lower jaw, besides fracturing my left eye socket. He never did knock me down, however. Guess I'm kinda proud of that fact. That heavyweight circled away from my power hand (right) and had a wicked overhand right himself. The Rock was a sadist. He liked to beat you mentally, with threats, in the locker room before the fight. He scared me so bad in the locker room that I nearly killed him in the ring.

The Rock, the ranked heavyweight, and Blackie, were all tough men. The scars you have seen on my face came from them, and men just like them. But I can honestly say they weren't tough enough to really hurt me. They were all predictable in the way they fought.

I knew what to expect from them, how they would react and where they were likely to hurt me the most. The scars they left on me no longer hurt. They are but reminders of another day.

The single toughest opponent I've ever faced, the most dangerous one—the one that truly hurt me the most and scares me yet today—is the one that beat me so badly that my entire family suffered from it. That same opponent killed the Rock, buried Blackie in an unmarked grave near the prison in Walla Walla, and has the heavyweight on a list for a liver transplant. That opponent is called "Addiction."

Oh, Addiction has a first name, several of them—all tough bastards too. Drug Addiction, Alcohol Addiction, Cocaine Addiction, Crack Addiction, and Heroin Addiction— to name a few. Addiction fights us all differently and is so slow and cunning you don't even know it's destroying you and your family. And worst of all, it will convince you that it's your friend, while getting you to drop your guard for a split second, so it can kill you. Yes, that's the toughest opponent I've ever faced.

If that's the opponent some of you readers are facing, I want to ask you to do me a favor. Read this carefully. I ask you to never give Addiction the chance to beat you like it beat me. I would ask you to recognize and never doubt for a second, the cunning of this murderous bastard. I would ask you to stay close to others who fight Addiction daily. Fight it in GROUPS as AA and NA teach us—NEVER ALONE. Never ever give Addiction a chance. Beat it for me and a million other people who have suffered its sadistic wrath.

You see, if you can help me teach young people how to beat Addiction, at this time in their lives, at their young age; not only have you rescued their entire family from Addiction, but you've paid for an insurance policy in full, which guarantees that they and their family will no longer suffer from the wrath of Addiction. I will have made a million guys just like me winners through you, in a fight with the most dangerous opponent I've ever faced.

So, do me this favor. Help me teach others how to win the fight against **ADDICTION,** and make us all winners.

MANY HATS

I seem to be many people these days. Some days just seem to take turns with my face and body. No mood lasts more than a few hours; continuity is gone. Alone in my cell, my mood is reflected in my writing or on the prison yard by whatever drama is brought to my attention.

A friend's story about his 70 year old mother slipping and falling in the parking lot at Washington State Penitentiary in Walla Walla, makes me angry. She had tried to see her son two times only to be turned back both times due to a dress code because her sweater didn't match her skirt. Finally, after a quarter mile walk back to her car, she fell down in tears, alone, her body exhausted.

I wrote a letter for a friend to the Parole Board in an effort to bring to light the terminal disease of another friend and his need to be given the opportunity to get proper medical treatment as a free person. This letter saddens me and makes some Church officials cry openly.

Waiting on a decision in another friend's case from the Ninth Circuit Court of Appeals, worries me. It causes me to doubt myself and wonder if I could have done more legally on his behalf. Defending a truly innocent man is hardest when one doesn't even know enough about what really happened to make up a good lie about it.

My grandson, (his Mother and Dad are going through a divorce), asks me why his Dad didn't get up to see him last weekend, on the day of their court-scheduled visit.

"Do you think Dad is mad at me, Grandpa?"

His Mother tells me that he has started wetting the bed. His Father is my son. And I, his Grandpa, would slap the tar out of his Dad if it weren't for this prison wall. Anger, guilt and heartache are using my body, because my son is doing the same thing I did a million years ago.

A prisoner tells me about his wife's address being stolen in some unknown manner. Another prisoner is now sending her dirty letters, wanting her to understand his sickness. There is anger in this husband's words. He has that right. He also wants to leave for work release any day now, so he is all but helpless to do anything about it. To react, would mean "hole time" and the loss of work release. I speak to the address thief. He shows me the letters she has written him back, inviting letters. I feel both anger and sympathy for the husband who doesn't know his wife.

A man tells me of sixteen hundred dollars missing from his work release account. DOC accounting knows nothing about it. He wants to know what can I do to help him..

"They can't do this, can they, Duke?"

In my mind I know they can and often do. But I tell him to file a Tort claim, and see what happens. For him, I try offer some hope of justice.

A young prisoner walking past my cell takes note of my daughter's picture. He asks if she would write him. My reaction is anger and I tell him,

"If my daughter wanted to write a punk or a loser, she would already be doing so."

The young passerby is not a punk nor a loser. It's his openly asking for my daughter's address that angers me. He may even be a nice young man. The hat of a guilt-ridden, over-protective father.

A friend passes almost unnoticed. He looks depressed, so I holler at him,

"Get a haircut, hippie!"

He looks up and smiles. We both needed that smile. Another old friend is depressed. When I see him, I ask if he had any idea of just how butt ugly he is? Old Mac stares at me for a second, then breaks out in a big red-faced smile and says,

"You are a sick puppy, Duke."

A friendly insult, it works every time.

Alone in my cell, my mind races. Less than a year to go. Freedom is just around the corner. Then what? No more special seat in the chow hall. Who will ask for my advice then? Will I end up on some skidrow, in a cheap hotel, eating in soup lines, unable to find work? How long before my grandchildren get too old to spend time with Grandpa? Will my own grown children even like me? After all we are really strangers. How can they possibly have any respect for an old socially retarded man they hardly know? Questions—hundreds of them—flash through my mind, questions I can't answer for myself.

I'm told to write about my experiences, both good and bad. Maybe I should tell of the six days I spent in a steel culvert in Texas, in a fetal position, so the acid in the galvanized metal wouldn't eat my skin. Or perhaps I should write about the smell of a angry water moccasin, as it was dragged over my body for the enjoyment of prison guards, and how that smell lingers on your body for days. Even soap and water won't take it off.

Verify what Abbott says in his book, *"The Belly Of The Beast."*—yes, men really do say, "Oh, no, please!," before they die after being stabbed.

Yes, and even the toughest prison guards, especially the toughest, get sodomized during a riot. Yes, the blood mist of a wounded man does take the oxygen out of the air, and yes it smells like salt. Tell of the rage I felt when I attacked an armed prison guard on horseback, with a garden hoe. And tell you how it felt when he shot me five times at close range.

Lots of stories to write about, and I'll do it someday. However, they all pale in memory to one of those extra super big hugs from a child, one of those hugs that make you kinda grunt.

Or what about being the world's best peanut butter and jelly sandwich maker? I *was* once, ya' know. I would spread newspapers on the floor, get the biggest jars of peanut butter and jelly I could find and we would all sit in a circle and just load up. Yep, that's what I want. My tombstone should read, Edward Allen Lee—The world's best peanut butter and jelly sandwich maker. Now, *that* is something to be truly proud of.

OF GRANDPAS AND DADDYS

Grandpas are better than Daddys—sometimes. Grandpas seem to have more time to fix bikes and stuff. They tell really good stories, too. Grandpas always give money too, not much though. And Grandmas are the best cooks in the world too, sometimes even better than Moms. Of course, Grandpas don't have to go to work as much as Daddys do, so they have more time at home, time to do good stuff. So, Grandpas are kinda cool, at least I always thought so. They are the bosses too, because Moms and Dads always listen to Grandpas and Grandmas.

Today, I'm a Grandpa. I missed all but eight years of being a Daddy. When I was supposed to be a Daddy, I was walking a prison exercise yard. My days were spent trying to learn to be a boxer, reading, fist fighting, being a bully and lying to myself and everyone around me. My nights were spent listening to hundreds of prisoners screaming to be heard from cell to cell, a constant reverberation. Concrete and steel—sound and bullets bounce off both. When the lights were finally put out, silence takes over. The talk dies down and men are alone with themselves. No more false images, no one to impress, just darkness and memories. Brutal honesty comes with darkness in prison. It's a time for prayer, thinking, and at times, tears. Prayers to be called Daddy, just one more time.

As the years rolled by, during visits, or on the telephone, Daddy became Dad. Then it was, "Dad, meet my wife," followed by, "Dad, how does it feel to be a Grandpa?" Today, I'm Dad, Grampa, Gumpagumpa, and still a Bombee, too. My oldest grandsons watch my old fight films and ask,

"Was that really you, Grandpa?"

Oh, there is one little one who still screams Gumpagumpa, whenever she hears my voice. And there's another who asks the one question that lets every Grandpa know he is the one to spend time with,

"Hey Grandpa, ya know what?"

The older ones are busy, they have girl friends and stuff to do. They don't have much time for Grandpa.

In 2001, I'll walk out of this prison cellblock, socially retarded, unsure, and scared—an old man in a strange world. I have no idea of what is and what isn't anymore. I'm not completely sure if my dreams and memories were ever real, its been so long. However, I hope to hear,

"Hey Grandpa, ya know what?"

That is, if time hasn't made that little one too busy for Grandpas too. Yes, I dream about fixing lots of bikes, giving little ones some money from time to time, not much though. And telling some stories to little faces with big eyes and open mouths. The problem is, when I get asked that best of all questions,

"Hey Grandpa, ya know what?"—this Grandpa doesn't know what. This Grandpa will never go along with....

"Dad, you move in with us," or "Bombee, you are going to stay with me and don't you dare say no!"

No, this Grandpa is too ashamed to show how socially retarded he has become. This Grandpa has learned to be alone, learned it well, especially during the Christmas holidays. Cissy's Bombee, is an institutionalized old convict to everyone but her. Guy and Troy's Dad is no longer a fearless boxer; he is a scared old man attempting to slip into society unnoticed. Besides, who ever heard of a real Grandpa who had never even seen a video game?

I know only about crime, prisons, corruption, and how they all support each other. It sure isn't a topic to discuss with my grandchildren. Camping can't have changed much. Guess I'll still know about that. But, talking about what I know and what I've lived, with my family, makes me feel like I'm dirtying them. In plain English, I'm ashamed of what I've lived, thus ashamed of what I know.

I'm going to do my best to be a good Grandpa. Nothing on this earth is more important to me. I paid one hell of a price to learn the value of being a **DADDY**. There ain't a chance in hell of me ever overlooking my second chance. That of being a **GRANDPA**.

THE OPPOSITE OF
WHAT'S SPOKEN

It goes without saying that there are many men in prison with explosive personalities, men who generate fear, men you kinda walk on eggshells around, so to speak.

Therefore, where I speak to the men I sit with in class, I often call them "the sick ones" or even sometimes, "assholes." It's a compliment. It tells them I am comfortable to speak unhindered around and about them; that I like and trust them.

I call most young men with long hair, "Hippies." I often throw some totally wild off-the-wall insult at one of them. I'm telling them the same thing, the same message. In fact, if I didn't like and trust this same person, I would address him only in a formal manner, and only when forced to. The same goes for the guards. If I'm comfortable around a guard, we trade insults—thus laughter.

I made a statement the other day in class about wanting to be smart and have high grade points, but that I was too dumb to select a good attorney to keep my ass out of the joint. That fit everyone of us. Few convicted men feel their attorney had done everything possible for them. The insult was there and it fits all of us.

When the hippies in class were laughing about my letter concerning the study of 2200 year old Greek homosexuals, they complimented me by telling me they trusted me enough to laugh at me. Several days later, when it was made plain that we were going to study the Greeks, the hippies were beside themselves with glee saying, "Old Duke ain't never gonna pass this course after the letter he wrote." Again, it was a compliment to me. Those hippies wouldn't be laughing and teasing me if they feared my reaction.

The reason I've used "I" so much in this writing is because "I" know what it's like to have men act phony around me, because they feared my reaction. I remember the days when "I" was so unstable mentally that if someone had made fun of me or teased me, "I" would have possibly broken their jaw. It feels damn good to be insulated with a smile and laughed at honestly. Yes, and even those goddamn Hippies pick on me. "I" wouldn't have it any other way these days.

THE MAKING OF MONSTERS

It's seen in operation daily in every prison in America; prisoners, angry people, deprived of more and more human rights as the clock ticks, people claimed by the state and forgotten. Prisoners are so abused, that *Amnesty International* now cites America for human rights violations. America, the land of the free, is also the land that incarcerates more of its citizens per capita than any other country on this planet. America's crime rate is looked at as no less than a war zone by many countries.

The new trend is "Prison Industries." Perhaps the old name is more accurate "Forced Labor." The difference is of course, that nowadays prisoners don't break rocks for the state. They make items used by Boeing, Starbucks, Nike, Ford Motors and many other major corporations. Prisoners are often sanctioned for being late or missing work. They lose good time for it or are even thrown in the hole. They work for minimum wage, less room and board set by the state, and another 35% deducted for general incidentals. It boils down to about a dollar or so per hour. It looks good on paper, but is little different than the forced labor camps of China in the respect that their freedom depends on the type employee they are.

There is an excellent argument for keeping prisoners busy. Make them work. Have them develop a work ethic because they have it too easy, anyhow. Good arguments all. The problem being, they are made by people with little knowledge of what actually happens inside today's prisons or with political idiots seeking public favor.

It isn't the prisoner who truly gets the shaft, it's the taxpayer. If a prisoner gets caught smoking a cigarette in a no smoking area in either Washington or Oregon for a third time, the taxpayer can pay a minimum of fifteen thousand dollars for that third cigarette—often does too.

Now you talk about the cost of tobacco! One year's good time can, and is, often taken from the prisoner for three infractions in a given period of time. Look it up; that year costs the taxpayer fifteen grand! And that's only the tip of this iceberg.

I've known prisoners to lose 180 days good time ($15,000.00, to the taxpayer), for some really dangerous contraband like a plastic coffee mug without his inmate number on it. Or, for having an unauthorized typewriter, too many out-of-date magazines, being late for work in prison industries, or possibly the most threatening act of all; having the audacity to tell a corrections officer he is wrong, even when it's true. Still, that isn't what really hurts the public.

No, what hurts the public are the monsters they are creating in this industry who are released back to an unsuspecting public.

Prisons today are no less than an industry, in and of themselves. A failed industry and possibly the biggest ongoing fraud ever perpetrated on the American taxpayer. It's no secret. Just look at the recidivism* rate, Over all, in a five year period, it's well over 77.7%. That's five out of every ten people sent to prison return (not only not corrected, but much more antisocial than when they came in). One must ask himself, just how much money will a sane taxpayer invest in an industry with a 77.7% failure rate? An industry geared to create angry, violent people for release on the unsuspecting taxpayer who foots the bill for it all?

If you want a shocking revelation, just look at the pictures of this prison industry's true finished product. Not the packages packed by inmates for Starbucks;, the Department of Correction's real finished product is the released inmate.

Compare the mug shots of inmates, when they first come to prison, with their release pictures. People come in scared, bewildered, unsure and in shock. Some so lonely they are crying. They leave with an education in anger and deceit, with callused emotions and socially retarded. The prisoner may come in crying but he will not leave that way, I promise you; the Department of Corrections will see to it.

The death rows of these two states (Washington & Oregon) are horrific mute proof of the callused emotions instilled by their respective prison industries.

There are very few men on death row who are not graduates of some prison industry....somewhere. What the Washington State taxpayer pays the Department of Corrections for (an 849 million dollar budget), is no less than to support a captive industry in—**THE MAKING OF MONSTERS.**

SIZE MAKES A DIFFERENCE

Several years ago, I was at a gathering of prisoners and their families in the prison visiting room. The prisoners have what is called a "Speaking Panel." It's a group of prisoners who speak to different groups of free people twice a month. The prisoners tell their stories and the free people ask questions. It's good in that it educates both groups.

Once a year, the institution lets the prisoners involved have a kind of party as a reward. They're allowed to invite family members from their approved visiting list to this party. It's about one of these gatherings that I now write.

As the families moved around visiting, I took note of a friend's little daughter. She was one of those little chubby kids that make you smile by just looking at her. Anyhow, she had this ice cream bar and she was really enjoying it. It was easy to tell she was enjoying it because she was saving part of it on her face. I watched this little ice cream eater for a few minutes and finally asked her,

"Can I have a bite?"

Well, she didn't know about *that* deal. She looked at me, then back at her ice cream bar, back at me, and said "Nope!"

So, I tried, "please, pretty please," begged a bit, groveling some, and done some first class sniveling. Still the answer was nope.

Finally I just pulled out all the stops. I balled up my fist, put it over my eye and let go with a loud, "Whaaaa." I was crying big time. That did it, she could stand no more.

So, she stuck out her precious ice cream bar to me for a bite and with one big growling snap, I got it, the whole thing and pulled all the ice cream off the stick! Man!—that cute chubby little lady gave me a look that would have made Mike Tyson crawl right out of the ring! She just threw the stick right at me, too! Then she attacked and even kicked me couple times. Finally, she backed up and told me in some kind of foreign, half-English threat, that I had better get her another ice cream bar, and get it quick!

Well, I know when I'm whipped. So, I got her another ice cream bar—Quick! However, every time she walked by me for the next hour or two, she kinda sheltered her ice cream bar from me, never failing to give me a look that said, "Back off, Buster."

I figure that I weigh about 250 pounds more than her, so you can see **SIZE ISN'T ALWAYS A MEASURE OF WHO IS THE TOUGHEST.**

POPCORN

What would I want if these prison doors were opened for me today? The first thing would be a small apartment, no more than two or three rooms, in a busy part of town so I can watch life from a safe distance. Besides food and clothing, a word processor, and maybe a few months down the road, a good used pickup to get around in and go camping with my grandchildren. That's it, nothing fancy, just a slow way to learn about the outside world at my own speed ... And eat some popcorn.

My dream is that I could make a living writing stories about my past. I've learned to speak in public fairly well, the result of being on the speaking panel for outside guests here in prison. We always spoke to people who had some law enforcement experience or people who were forewarned of the topics we would cover in our talks. I'm sure if I were to speak to a group of normal citizens, openly and honestly, shock would be a factor. I'll have to go slow and warn people ahead of time and not be totally honest in describing prison life.

A serial killer slept on the floor in my cell for about six months due to overcrowding. I feel that experience brought out both the worst and the best in me. He caused me many sleepless nights. Not out of fear of him—no,—it was the horror of his all-too-true stories. Stories of torturing young women all across the country. I found myself wanting to beat him badly. To give him the beating all those girls had taken from his big, cowardly hand. It got to the point where I actually tried to provoke him into taking a swing at me, so I would have an excuse to break his jaw.

This experience also woke me up to the fact that this serial killer and I were much alike. We were both ex-boxers, both truck drivers, both liked country music, shooting pool, drinking beer and we were both large men, well over six feet tall. The difference was, he laughed when he told stories about torturing his victims and I cried. Not in front of him, to be sure; I cried inside, alone in my bunk at night. After listening to his stories and finding how close he came to my own loved ones, it made me see just how much my own family meant to me.

I covered the horror of this killer's stories with memories of kindness and love. It woke me to how very special my family truly was. I buried what this killer told me under the important things in life. There has been a bunch of hate, violence, and anger in my life to be sure. There has also been a bunch of plain good honest love.

Memories of a little girl with big eyes and pigtails, sitting on my lap, feeding me popcorn one piece at a time, as I growled and snapped at her tiny fingers, playing like a monster, as she squealed in delight. Memories of a tiny sweating head, asleep on my chest, just plain zonked out because Bombee let her stay up too late, with popcorn all over the floor.

I used memories like that to cover the madness and pain I was hearing from this killer. I had to. If I had done anything else, I may well have talked myself into being a monster, seeking revenge for all those girls that died at that killer's hand.

It was the same little girl, with pigtails and big eyes, now a grown woman, that this killer bragged about seeing many times. He even told me how pretty my little Cissy was and how he had taken note of her and her mother as they waited on him from behind a lunch counter.

One day I asked the killer if he had any idea of what one of those two girls' lives were worth. I relayed to him that if he had hurt my daughter or her mother, and had the misfortune of being placed in the same cell with me ... Well, he could die a most unpleasant death.

He was shocked that I would even consider such a thing and was visibly shaken. For several days he kept his horror stories to himself. He told me that he could actually feel my anger in the air when I told him about killing him over Cissy or Sheri.

He asked to be moved out of my cell and was moved. Guess he had no idea that a Daddy can be a real life monster to anyone who would hurt a little popcorn feeder; yes, his worst nightmare in fact.

Today, I look back on my feelings at that time and they actually kinda scare me. I now look at things a bit different. My daughter and her mother never even knew just how close they came to a real live monster. I thank God for that. It's a hell of a thing to say,

"A serial killer woke me up to the truly important things in my life," ...but he did.

Today, I don't need a big fancy car, expensive home or even a high paying job. I need to surround myself with what has been there all this time—love, softness and caring. I need to write about those special memories, and I need more of them. I shudder when I think of how close that killer came to making me a killer and I wonder if all daddies who are snapping, snarling, popcorn eaters, are like that? Guess it's something in the **POPCORN**, huh?

DUCKING

I remember Mrs. Moen, my second grade teacher asking me one day,

"Why do you always duck and cover your head when I walk by?"

Guess I told her that I didn't know, basically because I didn't know. All I knew for sure was, that if a big person walked up on me suddenly, I closed my eyes and ducked, grabbing my head. Course, in those days I didn't know how to slip a punch, so as a rule I took the full force of anything coming my way.

Plus, I always closed my eyes and that is a no-no, because it causes a person to lose their sense of balance and down you go. In those days I didn't know many of these things so, out of instinct, when I was knocked down, I would either get up running or just curl up in a fetal position.

Now when I think about it, at least to the best of my knowledge, there is simply no way to slip a punch that comes from above. It comes in too hard to block with little arms, when the person throwing the punch is three feet taller.

Getting out of the danger zone is all but impossible. Most of the time the punch came out of nowhere. You just see a flash and BLAM...Down you go. It happens so fast it doesn't even hurt. Something in you screams, though. Not out of pain really, it's fear more than anything, fear and surprise. Your natural reflexes will cause you to cover your head and go down screaming.

Later, when it's over and you're alone you can check for what hurts....physically,that is. Most of the time the bruises don't last long. Little boys heal really fast. They can take one hell of a beating, you would be surprised. Guess it's because they're so flexible... physically, that is.

I was always glad when it was over and I was alone, so no one could see me because I was ashamed. I was always so sure those beatings were my fault and that I was lucky it wasn't a lot worse. Begging doesn't work. Those big people have heard all that, "Please don't hit me no more," stuff before. So, just take the beating and hope they will quit hitting you.

Yes, little boys can take one hell of a beating, you would be surprised... physically, that is.

* I don't know why I wrote this. Guess it's just something that I needed to tell someone. Not many people are three feet taller than me these days, so I don't duck and cover my head much any more. I was in high school before I quit ducking. By the time I got to prison and old Leo Dobbs taught me to slip a punch, it was too late anyhow. I didn't need to **DUCK** anymore.

CREATING A STRANGER

To make strangers of the wife and children you have spent the last several years with, go to prison. Slowly, no matter how hard you try, you will begin to get weekly supervised visits, from strangers. It starts with your family moving to some new and cheaper place to live. A place you know nothing about, a place you have never been. Then possibly the car you had, the one you were so proud of, is lost to the finance company; its replacement is totally unknown to you.

Your children will live in lower class neighborhood and attend different schools. They will speak of friends you never heard of. In time, your children grow and develop new habits, their personalities change. Your wife gets a new hair style. She is now forced to go to work. She has money problems you know nothing about. She tells you about neighbors you have never met and know nothing about. Your family soon talks of, works with, and goes to school with, people you've never met.

Your family will progress with time. They speak of higher prices and appliances and games now on the market that you have never heard of. You are under social arrest. You know nothing of the new cars coming out each year; nothing of wages or the cost of living and the problems facing the family you once knew everything about and understood so well.

You have become a stranger to them. You are harder to understand. Your temper flares more often and you can't relate to them like you once did. Finally, your conversation with them will become one of different values, strange friends and new goals. **STRANGERS HAVE BEEN CREATED.**

I HATE VISITING ROOMS

I was waiting in the Washington State Reformatory visiting room, waiting to see my attorney. The room was full of families visiting loved ones in prison. As I sat in the corner, next to the Attorney/Client visiting area, a little boy came and stood directly in front of me, about an arms length away. He just stood there staring at me, three fingers in his mouth and his nose running a little. Finally, after a minute or two, he said,

"You got big feet."

"Ya think so, huh?," I answered, surprised.

"See?," he said, coming close and putting his little sneaker next to my size 14, prison issue boot.

"Yep, guess I have," I said, as we both looked in agreement at the difference in the sizes of our shoes.

"My Daddy says you are mean," he said.

"He does, huh? What's your Daddy's name?," I ask.

"David. He's right over there; do you see him?"

Then I heard the little boy's Dad say,

"Allen, you quit bothering Duke," and then he tells me,

"If he is bothering you, Duke, just run him off."

I looked at the little boy. His fingers were back in his mouth again as he waited to see if he would get run off or not.

"He ain't bothering me," I told the boy's Dad.

Then, looking at the little boy, I said,

"So, your name is Allen, huh?"

"Yeah," he answered. "I can run fast too, ya' know. Do you wanna see?"

"Yeah, let me see how fast you can run," I tell him as he takes off, down to the Coke machine and back.

"Yep, you're a fast one," I tell him as he stands there puffing proudly.

"What's your name?, " he asks.

"Eddy," I tell him. He thinks it over for a few seconds, takes a deep breath and seems satisfied with my name.

"Do you like banana splits Allen?," I ask?

"Yeah."

"With nuts on it?"

"Yeaah!"

"An' whipped cream?"

"Yeeaah!"

"An' cherries too?"

"Yeeaaah!"

"An' chicken noodle soup on it too?"

"Yuk! Uggaah! Nobody does that; puts noodle soup on banana splits. Yuk. Gross!," he says with a wrinkled-up nose.

Then we both start laughing. Soon Allen's Dad tells him to be quiet. We try to quit giggling but it does no good.

About then I smell a foul odor. Someone has passed gas in the area. I motion to Allen to come closer and whispered in his ear.

"Smells like somebody pooped their pants," I told him.

That did it! Allen tried to stop giggling by putting both hands over his mouth. He was literally squeaking as he tried to hold the sound in. Then Allen's Mom asked him what was wrong with him; why was he being so noisy. It did absolutely no good; he couldn't quit laughing, nor could I. It was, in fact, the best laugh I've had in years.

My attorney walked up as Allen and I were trying to quit giggling. When Allen saw him, he became quiet immediately. He moved over beside me and put his little hand on my knee, as he looked my attorney up and down closely, three fingers back in his mouth again. Out of reflex or instinct, I put my big beat up hand over Allen's hand on my knee. Again, Allen and I agreed on something; he didn't like those damn attorneys either.

Something came over me, something like an almost forgotten dream. An awful feeling of something dear, rediscovered. I had to get out of that room. I stood and told my attorney to get Allen a candy bar as I left, going as fast as I could towards the Attorney/Client room.

My attorney looked surprised and said something like,

"Okay Duke, are you all right?," as I walked off. When I got to the door, I heard a tiny voice at full volume saying,

"Goodbye, Eddy."

I turn and wave saying,

"Good bye, Allen."

Then it hits me. It's those tiny trusting little hands. I had forgotten how they felt. How often had I felt the soft little hands of my own children on my knee and felt the unquestioned trust in them. So long ago... How long had it been since I'd had a totally unguarded and simply honest talk with a child? My God... Had my time in prison robbed me of even the memory of softness and trust? Had I forgotten the feeling of good honest laughter and the touch of tiny trusting hands?

After finishing my business with my attorney, I returned to my cell for a very tough night filled with memories of tiny trusting hands and how much I missed the touch of a child. The next day I was walking the prison yard when I came across Allen's dad.

"Was the rug rat bothering you yesterday Duke?," he asked.

"Thought his name was Allen!," was my angry retort.

"Oh yeah, it is. It's just a saying; it don't mean nothin'," he said.

"Kids ain't rug rats; they got names," I said, still angry.

"Okay Duke,—hell, it's just a figure of speech. By the way, how come Allen called you Eddy, Duke?"

"Cause I used to be an Eddy, an' maybe he knows me better than you do," was my honest and still angry answer.

Damn, **I HATE VISITING ROOMS**, especially those in prison. They're just too full of honest feelings.

A WORDLESS GIFT

Who truly thinks in words? Being bilingual, I have been asked if I think or dream in English or Norwegian. I don't believe that my thinking process involves words of any type. My thinking is a series of recognized feelings that are translated to a primitive form of grunts, groans, and screams, called words. In an effort to share these feelings with other humans who translate feeling to sound, I make noise that can be understood in two languages.

Dreams are but subconscious feelings and hallucinations. Our true helplessness comes from our inability to adequately express feeling with sound. Happiness may be a series of screams and squeals. Yet true, deep happiness, may be seen through tears, normally the reaction of fear and sadness. Thus, our attempts to communicate becomes truly a witch's brew of feelings and sound. Some sounds, not words, can truly invoke wonderful feelings.

I recall hearing children's voices, screams and squeals, coming from over the prison wall, as I sat alone in the Big Yard, early one Sunday morning. The wall, of course, blocked my view of these little sound makers. My immediate reaction was to close my eyes tightly and listen to each tingling sound. To try to capture this wonderful sound and to shut out everything else, feel the joy of it, relish it, hold it for just a few seconds more, behind tightly compressed eyes.

What words these children were saying made no difference to me. The free unguarded feeling their sound transmitted to me was something I desperately wanted to hold on to. Sounds, thoughts of joy, the unexpected reward of sentiment, truly, **A WORDLESS GIFT.**

N.C.I.C V.S. HEART

For decades Law Enforcement Authorities have tried to figure out how one man who has been in prison can recognize another, almost on sight. To compensate for their failure to do this, the Justice Community spent millions of dollars setting up a National Criminal Identification Center (NCIC).

What isn't registered in the NCIC computers would fill volumes and will never be registered therein. It is the positive feelings of love and honor in the hearts of people that authorities have condemned as old convicts, career criminals, and even dirt bags, in today's language. The anger and futility felt by officials is evident in their negative, immature name-calling, even today.

A bond equally as strong as that of blood brothers is often formed between friends forced, by error or belief, into combat or prison. It happens to people who experience danger, fear, and pain together; people forced to eat, sleep, bath, and even go to the bathroom together. People who take the time to know each other's likes, dislikes, and secrets, and, out of respect, will even share pain with one another to the point of tears.

Experiencing these things forms a brotherhood, a union that's secured by unquestioned loyalty. Some of us were born in suffering, now we are all computerized outcasts, brothers in loneliness, hated, and feared by the authorities.

Yet, we are true to one another. We have been forced to test life to its fullest as prisoners or warriors. We no longer feel comfortable with the boredom normal life offers. We have seen the permanent quickness of death and now some even find a type of rightness in the open violation of society's rules. Restless, antisocial criminals and warriors, we are recognized and understood only by one another.

The million dollar computer claims to know us well, yet I'm actually unsure of who I am. Am I the angry convict the NCIC computers say I am, or a grandfather whose dream is to go camping and fishing with his grandchildren? Am I a heartless criminal portrayed by the computer, or the protector of animals, children, and those I love? Would I fight for a convict friend, even to the point of death, or am I hard and uncaring. Have I cried in pain, loneliness, and shame, alone in a dark prison cell, silently wishing for another chance, and hoping for what could have been, or am I devoid of conscience?

The computer doesn't know the answers to these questions, thus the authorities can't figure out how we know each other. I doubt if we ourselves could fully explain how we recognize one another. To the eye and camera, we look like every other citizen of this country. The media often pictures convicts as flat-nosed with cauliflowered ears—stupid humanoids to get tax dollars for, by instilling false images in the mind of the public.

Could it be that our hearts recognize the pain, loneliness and shame in others because we've shared it with one another? If feelings can't be programmed into computers, (especially that million dollar **NCIC** computer), will that expensive computer ever have the **HEART** to truly know us?

STRANGULATED HERNIA

"Strangulated hernia" is what the Doctors say can happen to my friend Sammy. When the stomach muscles slam shut on an exposed hernia, it happens. Guess it's dangerous too. Sammy is doing plenty of sniveling, anyhow.

Here I am on my hands and knees scrubbing the floor in my cell. I'm the one who should be sniveling. You never see those convicts in the movies scrubbing floors, doing their laundry, or crawling around on their knees, rear-end straight up in the air like I am right now. I bet old Jimmy Cagney would never go for it. It's just plain embarrassing.

Wonder how they make those TV prison cells look so big. My cell is the same size as two regular double mattresses side by side. Course, I've also got a toilet, sink. table, stool, and bunk in that area. Then, there is all my shampoo, clothing, books, and if I don't smoke, drink coffee, or buy postage stamps, and save every single penny I earn on my prison job for six months, hell; I can put a TV in the cell too.

Smells are a problem living in close quarters like this. As you walk past each cell, the odor of instant coffee, cigarette smoke, shampoo, dirty bodies, smelly feet, bad breath, or any fool with a gas problem, introduces you to the cell's resident. The latter has either a temporary problem, or will no doubt reside in the infirmary area.

We have recycled air, too. Saves money, ya know. They don't have to reheat or cool the air if they recycle it. Course, if the inmate three tiers below you, and 20 cells away starts coughing with some lung problem or hoof and mouth disease, rest assured the air now in his distant cell will replace the air in yours within minutes. Yes, these modern methods of conservation purely overwhelm me at times. If they ever find out that AIDS is an airborne disease, the prison population will soon be nil.

Canteen is always the highlight of the week. Most of us work for $52.00 per month. That's about one hour per postage stamp, just in case you still want to write someone. An old Bic pen costs about two hours work, a writing tablet four hours and a bag of Keefe coffee is a little over a day's pay. Prison economics. Going to sick call now costs over a day's wage. Yes, with that recycled air, the old sick call is a regular little moneymaker.

We got it made in prison, they say. In the papers they call them Country Clubs. With what I've seen on TV about prisons, it's no wonder the public thinks this place is a bed of roses. Sheer unending boredom, concrete and steel, life in a closet. Sound and bullets bounce off everything in these cell blocks, except us. That's the truth about doing time. A person grows so small in time. So angry at watching your loved ones slowly become strangers, so ashamed of the pain his family tries to hide at each visit, that, in time, he is unsure of who he himself is. He even becomes a very angry stranger to himself.

I don't want to forget to tell you about that two mattress-size cell of mine. It's got one wall missing, too. There are only bars cover that wall so you can see right in there anytime.

It's for security reasons. They also have female guards here, which makes for some truly rushed feelings when one of them comes to hand me my mail, when I'm on the throne answering the call of nature. That could cause a **STRANGULATED HEMORRHOID**.

THE VALUE OF A WORD

Words have tremendous value. I was raised on a farm in northeastern North Dakota in the early 1950s. My first month in a little rural schoolhouse taught me a lesson that I value yet today.

My friend Don Holmes and I were having a crab apple fight during recess one day. The Teacher caught me just as I threw an apple at Don. Well, she got mad and made me come back into the schoolhouse. She told me how wrong it was to throw apples at other people and how badly someone could be hurt. 'Course, by this time I was pretty embarrassed and ashamed of what I had done. Then, she told me that she wanted me to apologize to Don in front of the whole class.

When the rest of the kids came in from recess, the teacher called me to the front of the class, explained to everyone what I had done, and told me to apologize to my friend Don.

However, I just stood there with my head down, in front of the class and did nothing, too ashamed to even talk. The Teacher told me to apologize again. I just stood there in shameful silence, staring at the floor. Then the Teacher took a ruler and smacked me on the head and told me once again to apologize to Don.

Now, besides being embarrassed and ashamed, I started to silently cry, as I stared at the floor, in front of everyone. The Teacher then smacked me again, even harder, as I stood silently with tears streaming down my face.

Finally, she just gave up and told me to remain standing in front of the class until I apologized. So, I stood there, spending the longest day of my life, in shame, crying in silence, and staring at the floor in front of the whole school.

When school was over, the teacher told me that I had to stay after everyone else left. When they were gone, she came up to me and asked me why I wouldn't apologize to Don, and why was I so stubborn. She went on to tell me that she didn't want to hit me with the ruler. She even said she felt bad for hitting me, but she had no choice because I was so stubborn.

Well, I told her not to feel bad because the ruler really didn't hurt that much anyhow, because I didn't want her to feel bad.

Then she asked me again, "Why are you so stubborn? Why won't you tell Don you are sorry?"

So, I asked her if that was what "apologize" means.

Then my Teacher, started crying too.

You see, if that Teacher had told me to tell my friend that I was sorry, I would have known what she meant, and would have done it instantly. I would have done almost anything to escape being made to stand crying, in shame, in front of my whole school. Knowledge of **WORDS** is so important, because words **HAVE TREMENDOUS VALUE.**

GUILT FREE

I live under a microscope, my every move monitored. There are rules for when and where I may take a shower, what and when I can eat, how I will dress, rules against expressing emotion, rules that dictate when and for how long I may sleep and even rules about when and where I can use the toilet. In fact, I must be visible to total strangers when taking showers and using the toilet.

Living under this microscope with the fear of being penalized for the smallest of these rule infractions is a constant companion. I have developed a want or need to enjoy a misdeed. Perhaps it's the harshness of my environment, the hardness of my surroundings or possibly a true need to witness the freedom of rule violation.

I crave the sight of a bumbling, happy, untrained puppy. I need to feel the puppy's freedom, softness and non-judgmental presence. His world is completely free. Only nature's rules are respected by the puppy. He goes anywhere he takes a notion to go. He experiences everything. He smells, tastes, chews on and tests everything he finds. He has no interest in the cold, hard, odorless and tasteless microscope.

Then happily, with sparkling eyes and happy face, in your full view, he will shit on the whitest of your expensive carpets... **"GUILT FREE."**

IT CAN ONLY GET WORSE

If I were a tax paying citizen today and had not done close to thirty years in prison, I'm sure my views of the world would be much different. I've always spoken out about the wrongs I've witnessed within the Corrections systems of the three states I've been incarcerated in. It may surprise many to hear that after all the wrongs done by me personally, I still attack wrongs whenever the chance arises. That's not to brag, my prison record is evidence of it.

My record shows transfers, segregation time, job losses, and reprimands, for what is called officially, "P.I." or Political Influence, meaning they have felt at times that I've had too much influence over other inmates attempting to change the system.

Having explained that, and had I not known the inside of a prison, my reaction to today's crime problems would possibly be much harsher than the average tax paying citizen.

For instance, abuse of a child should be taken out of the Criminal Justice System (where pedophiles are ware-housed for a few years and then released to re-abuse), to a Civil Commitment Court, where they can be committed to an institution for treatment, to include surgical procedures, until a board of Medical Professions, can be sure this offender will never reoffend.

I don't believe that I would accept the percentage of the cure that is now used. When some official tells me that a proven child molester has a 35% chance of not offending again, it's not good enough. Federal, as well as European, studies show that over 90% of pedophiles will not reoffend if surgically castrated.

Either cure the problem permanently, or commit the person until methods to do so are available. We spend an awful lot of money on research for serious illness. This sickness can be cured.

If their own numbers are looked at honestly, in regards to property crimes, burglary, theft, robbery, and many times fraud, they show plainly the overwhelming majority of these crimes are committed by people addicted to drugs or alcohol. Again, to warehouse these people does very little good. As a matter of fact, it possibly makes the problem worse.

During the warehousing, these offenders learn new tricks, continue their use, and regain their health for another shot at society. As inhumane as it sounds, I would suggest that addicts of drugs and alcohol, be isolated or committed, to some type of controlled living area, and the addiction fed.

Instead of spending twenty eight thousand dollars of taxpayers money per year warehousing these people, spend it on the drugs and booze they commit crime to get. Give them all they want, and food stamps to live. Make the criteria for acceptance to a rehabilitation program damn near impossible to gain. Then sit back and watch.

Many will die. Maybe even the majority will die, but one way or the other, society's problem is cured. Leave it to the addict. Live or die. Take your choice. Medical experts tell us addiction to drugs or alcohol is a life threatening disease.

Well then damn it, treat it like one, cure it one way or the other. Quit spending tax dollars to get them healthy and stop giving them the time to learn better ways to commit more crime.

As for sex offenders, we have the scientific data, results of experiments, and tried and proven methods to stop sex offenders for years. European studies show great success in this area. They have developed drugs, they use surgery, and they have all but cured the problem.

The single proven method that is a full-time failure, is warehousing them in prison, then releasing a better educated, healthier, pervert back into society.

Incarceration as punishment works. Incarceration as a form of rehabilitation has never worked, and it never will. You cannot teach a violent person to be nonviolent by housing him in a violent atmosphere for years. The majority of the programs in American prisons today, do little but create a bigger drain on tax dollars.

You have to accept the fact that it's not possible to teach a mentally sick, violent predator to get well. You have to cure the bastard. Corrections Officials are failing 77.7% of the time. Perhaps it's time to give Medical Professionals a shot at it.

With killers—violent, cold-blooded killers—it's simple; get rid of them. Why worry about how you do it? Chances are the bastard didn't worry about how the victim died. The public has to face the fact that there are human beings who are little more than walking bodies. They have no feeling for themselves or anyone else, so treat them exactly like that.

Take what useful organs they possess and bury the rest. At least someone would benefit besides Attorneys. People have to get the idea that murder is the ultimate crime, the worst crime that can be committed, out of their heads. Equally as bad, or possibly worse, is any crime that so injures a person mentally or physically, that it handicaps another for life. I believe life can be worse than death.

Now, I'll use the hard figures pertaining to my own case, breaking it down to taxpayer cost. I've never been arrested sober—never—not once. Safe to say, I am an alcoholic. I've been in three different state prisons for a total of over twenty eight years. At an average cost to the taxpayer of twenty seven thousand dollars per year, that's $783.000.00, or near that figure. Cold hard facts are, if the state had spent 10% of that figure on booze and food stamps, I would either be dead or would have worked damn hard to get into a rehab program in order to live. Either way, I would no longer be a drain on tax dollars, thus a crime statistic.

Now that I've written all my ideas about this matter, it's only fair to mention why this cold-blooded approach can't be done. First off, Prisons have become a very big business today, an easy way to get tax dollars from a scared and angry public.

Second, the Justice Systems all across this country have broken down and have been so for years. Crime is big business, big money, to this broken system. On a death-sentence case, an appeal Attorney is going to make in excess of a million dollars. It actually costs more to kill someone in this country than it does to incarcerate that person for life. The reason is very clear. To insure that no innocent person is murdered by the state. And that is exactly why these permanent solutions for crime can't be used in this country.

Our Justice System is so broken, they themselves clearly doubt the guilt of many they convict. Thus, Prosecutors and Police, having little to lose, often convict people by adjusting evidence to fit the crime. Until those who falsely convict others are themselves held criminally accountable for their actions, justice will continue to be a sellable item in this Country.

The fact is, there are many innocent and wrongly convicted people doing time in prisons all across America today, at taxpayer expense. Not rich people, not politically powerful people, and not people who can afford to fight for their rights.

A person can get as much justice as he or she can pay for in the United States today. Many guilty people, with money and political connections, walk free as a result. As long as "Justice For All, Beyond a Reasonable Doubt", and "Equal Protection Under The Law" are believed to be true by society and practiced by our Justice System, the public will pay for innocent people in prison, while guilty people are free to recommit crimes.

The O.J. Simpson trial is proof of this statement. How many murder trials have Five Defense Attorneys? How many last over a month, and how many people can pay six million dollars to defend themselves? Our justice System is broken, it has deteriorated to the point where on National Television, they show the World they don't offer equal protection under the law, and, **IT CAN ONLY GET WORSE!**

ALL OVER AGAIN

People often ask me what there is to write about. I see so many stories to write about. Unguarded stories, stories of heart and courage, stories told daily by actions—not words, and silent stories of true courage told by people in pain.

Not long ago a wheelchair-bound writer took the time to bashfully show me some poetry he had written. It was beautiful poetry with so much feeling and grace in his words. Not a word of self pity, nothing about can or can't do, only words from his heart. As I walked away after reading his poetry, I felt shame for the way I had always taken for granted the use of my hands and even complained about how clumsy they were at times.

I felt a deep respect for the trouble this man in the wheel chair had gone through just to type a single word. Pushing one key at a time with a shaky unstable finger, day after day. In fact, the poetry he had written could only be done by someone with true raw courage.

His poetry made me realize that it takes much more courage for the man in the wheelchair to write his feelings on paper, than it ever took for me to crawl into any boxing ring, against the toughest or most dangerous of opponents. What he has is real courage. The courage to keep going against all odds, and still he has the guts to come back tomorrow, to do it **ALL OVER AGAIN.**

ASSUMED LIBERTIES

Every time anyone comes to visit me, I'm subject to a strip search of my body when the visit is over. That means I'll have to remove all my clothing, bend over naked and spread my butt cheeks so some guard can inspect my rectum close-ly. Then I'll have to lift my scrotum and allow this guard to closely examine my crotch area also. It's a very embarrassing, degrading, ongoing practice, in almost every prison in Washington State. Many Federal Courts have ruled against this procedure over the years.

See: Hurley v. Ward, 549 F. Supp. 174 (S.D.N.Y. 1982); Frazier v. Ward, 426 F. Supp. 1354, 136066 (N.D.N.Y. 1977); Hodges v. Klein, 412 F. Supp. 896 (D.N.J. 1976), to name a few, yet the procedure continues. Corrections Officials assume the Liberty of doing as they see fit under the guise or name of "Security." Medical Experts, testifying in: Bell v. Wolfish, supra note 396, at 55660; Montana v. Commissioner's Court, 659 F. 2d 19 (5th Cir. 1981) or Olsen v. Klecker, 642 F.2d 1115 (8th Cir. 1981), stated flatly that visual inspection of the anal area of a person would prove fruitless even if that person had secreted something in their anal canal. The contraband, once past the sphincter muscle, is in fact invisible even to trained and professional medical personal. This degrading procedure is in fact used for its value as a tool of humiliation, more so than security. They assume the Liberty of violation of Federal Law, pure and simple.

This assumption of Liberty also includes a prisoner's family, if they come to visit. Anyone visiting a prisoner can be asked to submit to a strip search at any time. If they refuse, the visit is terminated. Courts haven't been asked yet if the family of a prisoner has the legal right of visitation. If and when they are asked, the assumption of liberty with family members will no doubt be treated the same by Corrections Officials.

I refuse to allow anyone to assume anything about my loved ones. I have no one on my visiting list that's truly important to me. I take the liberty of assuming that I can maintain a relationship with my loved ones by telephone and letter, thus removing the threat to me and of my family becoming victims of this state's illegal assumptions. Corrections Officials, may share only the **ASSUMED LIBERTIES** of kissing my family's collective Norwegian posteriors.

WORDS

Just imagine a world without words. Everyone judged by their actions, their deeds, as seen, not heard. No lies, no excuses, no promises—only silent deeds. Words, when used alone are, at best, poor inadequate tools for communication.

While the eye may see the brilliant sparkle of a diamond, words warn of cheap zirconium. Words can say, "it doesn't hurt," while the eyes cry. Words can say, "I don't care anymore," while the heart breaks, and words can say, "I'm not scared," while the hands shake.

We have no words to explain the feeling a person gets when a toothless, smiling, sparkling-eyed little baby, is held in our arms. Words can't begin to explain the emotion felt in a first love or a broken heart. Even the words, "speechless in love and horror," can't match the feelings of a parent watching a child being escorted out of a Courtroom, on the way to prison.

BRIGHT ORANGE COVERALLS

Going to the funeral of someone you dearly love is a traumatic experience, no matter how you cut it. Going to a funeral as a prisoner is beyond traumatic.

The convict is taken in chains and stiff bright orange coveralls, with no underwear, bare footed in rubber thongs, with a prison guard on each arm. Those bright orange coveralls seldom fit right. They tend to ride up in your crotch, being you have no underwear on, and they make you really stand out in the crowd. Your hands are chained securely to your waist by a belly chain with cuffs attached. But that's not the worst part.

Your feet can be moved only 14 inches due to the leg irons on your ankles, so you will walk in short shuffling steps. Then your feet will sweat, causing them to slip in those rubber thongs. With your hands secured at your side, these slipping thongs cause you to walk in a stumbling fashion, as the chains rattle. But, that's not the worst part.

The Chapel the funeral is held in is a quiet reverent place. A place where people dress in dark mourning clothes and share their grief in silence. Entering that sanctum, in front of your friends and relatives, under armed guard, in rattling chains, shuffling in shame, is hard to do. But that's not the worst part.

The worst part comes when the prisoner is ushered to the front of the Chapel, in front of everyone, to view the body of his loved one beside two uniformed prison guards. The prisoner can feel everyone staring at his shuffling form as he stands looking at the remains of his loved one. Then, when he turns to be led out of the Chapel, comes the worst part. The chains around the prisoner's waist stop his hands from even wiping the tears away. So he turns from the coffin, in tears, in front of everyone dear to him, and tries to hide his shame as he leaves.

Yes, that's the worst part of a visit to a funeral in **BRIGHT ORANGE COVERALLS.**

THAT OLD HEN

I was taking some college courses a while back, more to combat boredom than anything else. Seems some researchers from a University down south were studying response to different kinds of external stimuli, involving this chicken. They took this old hen and put her in a cage with a copper plate covering half the floor.

When the old hen wandered onto the part of the floor with the copper plate, an electric shock was administered. The old hen would naturally then jump back to the safe area, away from the copper plate. Shocked (I guess) is the word. Of course, the old hen forgot many times and wandered back to the copper plate, where she got another shock and jumped and ran to safety again. I imagine that old hen stepped on that plate a few times just to test it too.

I remember thinking at the time that it was really a hell of a way to treat an old hen. Lock the poor thing up in a cage and then shock the hell out of her when she walked around in it too much.

That shock kind of reminded me of the difference in your world outside these prison walls and mine inside. I get comfortable in my cell. I had a television, radio, pictures of my family all over the place and a prison job that paid 22 cents an hour, three squares and a hot shower every day. Can't beat that, not in my world anyway.

I can mail a letter for an hour and half's work, buy a Bic pen for four hours work, bag of cheap instant coffee for a little over a days pay. I don't even want to try and figure how many hours I had to work to pay for the television or radio. Ain't nothing free in prison. As a matter of fact, the cost is very high on most things.

I saw the shocked look on my 70 year old father's face when the metal detector malfunctioned and he had to be pat-searched in front of fifty strangers before he could see me. I also saw the shock and anger on my daughter's face when she was told she couldn't hold my hand during a visit, and that she could hug me only at the start and finish of our visit. So, I talked it over with my family and we agreed to write often, talk on the telephone weekly and visit only on special occasions. Like that old hen, I jumped to the safe area.

I learned to live well in this cell with all my pictures, much better these days, when I don't have to worry about my loved ones being exposed to and shocked by prison officials, just to see me. Then I no longer have to endure a complete strip search after every visit—no exceptions.

I could take it, but my family didn't have to take it, however. I had to, because it's just part of my world. My grandson doesn't understand why he can't sit on Grandpa's lap. Of course, he doesn't know how important security really is. He *does* know that he doesn't like guards or anyone in uniform, after all the times that even *he* has been shocked while visiting me.

Oh yes, talking about that old hen. Well, she and I are alike in another response. Ya see, those researchers went further with their experiment. After they got that old hen used to half the floor being safe and half being a shocking experience, they made the whole floor copper. They shocked that old hen no matter where she stood.

Do you know what that hen did then? Well, she just sat down. She gave up on moving anywhere, for any reason, no matter how much electricity they shocked her with. I'm kinda like that old hen.

Still, it's a hell of a way to treat an old hen, don't ya think? I wonder if **THAT OLD HEN** would act different if they told her it was for security reasons.

NOT ALLOWED IN PRISON

"Ya know Duke, when I'm around people who know that I've done time in prison and something goes wrong or gets stolen, I just start feeling guilty 'cause I'm thinking they are gonna suspect me of doing it anyhow. Don't make no difference if I did it or not. I still feel guilty 'cause those people know I done something wrong before. Do ya know what I mean, Duke?"

"Yes, I know the feeling," I said in answer to the old convict's question.

He had just returned to prison for a parole violation (drinking), and was feeling depressed. Some money had been stolen from the business he was working for and he got scared or paranoid, said to hell with it, and took off on the run. A warrant was put out on him and he was arrested several months later in Oregon.

He was drunk when arrested so that became his violation. The missing money was found and the person who took it was put in jail. His first mistake wasn't taking off on the run; it was not taking a good look at himself when he first got out of prison.

While in prison, it's almost impossible to take a good personal inventory of oneself, because the decision making process has been removed from your life. You are a number.

You are alone. Your friends, family and neighbors don't even exist. Every minute thing you do is done at the ringing of a bell, the command of an officer, or the clanging of a metal door opening and slamming shut. You have become an inmate, the system accepts nothing less.

A person has to rediscover himself when he leaves prison. Some of us, due to addiction, have buried the person we really are, under so many years of mind-altering chemicals and numbed feelings, that we hardly even remember who or what we were.

Sometimes it means becoming almost childlike, because childhood was the last time we were really honest with ourselves. Then, if you are able to peel back all those layers of abuse and numbness, you may find out that the person that you spent so much time covering up, escaping from and hiding from, was a pretty special person. Perhaps even a person you would like and respect. Someone you would like to be. You can find the real you, but honesty must be your goal.

To attempt something this open and honest while in prison would open a person up to ridicule and harassment. It would, in fact, make you an outsider in the prison environment. To survive in prison, one must first recognize the fact that honesty and openness are forbidden—not allowed—and that the punishment for being so, can and will often result in death.

Prisons are designed for failure. Their goal is not to teach honesty. It is to harden your emotions and create failure. Your first lie is, "I'm #242523; I no longer have a name." It's **NOT ALLOWED IN PRISON.**

MERCY OF A GIANT

After being in prison for over twenty years, the question I'm asked most often is about fear. Questions like,

"Aren't you afraid in prison? Weren't you scared?"

Surprisingly, the most and greatest fear I've ever experienced was prior to my eighth birthday. Fear is a constant companion in prison. However, the violence that causes that fear is seldom expected, is generally quick, over in a heartbeat, and totally unexpected. With little warning, a person has very little to worry about. Therefore, fear of real violence in prison is short lived.

As a child I knew true fear. Fear of what was a giant to me at the time, a god with total control of me. In reality, the fear of a parent and the violence he could inflict. For instance, I learned that an eight year old boy could be knocked unconscious after being hit in the back with a thrown hammer—a full week after the blow was struck.

It happens when the boy is told to go get a certain type hammer and he returns with the wrong one. The adult then screams and throws the hammer. The little boy sees the hammer coming, turns his back and covers his head in fear, taking the full force of the blow.

The hammer hits him squarely in the back, but the boy doesn't really feel the pain; he's too scared. He runs to hide as fast as a little person can, with the wind knocked out of him, and hides in the trees. There alone, he can cry and feel the pain, because no one can see him—he is safe.

In a few days however, the little boy's leg starts hurting. But being afraid of the giant, he says nothing. He still cries alone in the trees behind the machine shop. The pain gets worse. A week later, the boy can't even walk up and down the stairs to his bedroom; he crawls because the leg hurts terrible. He even waits until his little sister is not around, for fear she will tell the giant that he can't walk up the stairs.

Then one morning after the boy crawls down the stairs, he tries to stand up and he passes out. He wakes up in the hospital. The Doctor tells the parents that the little boy has a badly bruised kidney and that he has developed a severe infection. The little boy is scolded for not being more careful when climbing trees, because they say he hurt himself climbing trees.

The little boy is happy, however. He is safe. He doesn't fear the adults in the hospital. He will be safe for two whole weeks. So, you see, an eight year old boy can be knocked unconscious, with a body blow, a week after it happens.

I remember my younger sister and I going to town one day with the giant, in a big farm truck. At the grain and feed store, we were told to go sit in the corner, out of the way, while the adults loaded the truck. Hanging on the wall, above our heads, were big clusters of brightly colored plastic rings, the kind used on chicken's legs as a color code marking. Several of these plastic rings had fallen on the floor where my sister and I were sitting. We picked them up and tried the different colors on our fingers. We finally selected one each.

After the truck was loaded, the lady who worked at the feed store came and gave us each a red Red Hot jawbreaker, "for being so good and staying out of the way," she said.

That night at the supper table, one of the giants noticed the plastic rings on our fingers. He instantly became angry and sent us both upstairs to bed. A few minutes later, we were confronted by the screaming giant with an electrical cord in his hands.

I don't remember much of the beating, mostly just the screaming, but I woke up in the middle of the night, stuck to the sheets. I remember crying silently, in fear, as I slowly pulled those stuck sheets off my back and legs. I was sure another beating was forthcoming because I had got blood on the sheets.

After I got the sheets off my body, I rolled them up in a tight ball and smuggled them outside into the trees behind the machine shop and hid them. For several months after that, yet another fear was added to my world. I feared the giants would someday find the sheets I had ruined with my blood.

Today, at 6'5 and 270 pounds, it's much harder to whip me with an extension cord or knock me out with a body blow. And yes, I've known fear in prison, but never have I known such fear as I lived with as a child, at the **MERCY OF A GIANT.**

FEAR ADDICTION

I believe that when a man lives with fear on a daily basis, for years together, he kinda gets addicted to it. Prison is fear oriented. You fear losing good time, visits, your property, your friends, and even your life. The system has taken it upon itself to generate fear daily. To totally relax and enjoy anything is next to impossible.

Tonight, I heard a young man talk about an infraction report that had been written on him in the visiting room. It seems that his wife had the nerve to deliberately violate the visiting room rules by placing her hand on this man's shoulder for a period of 3 minutes. The Sergeant-in-charge had timed this deliberate act and told the officer to write an "Infraction Report." The next step is, of course, possible suspension of his visits for a given period of time by the hearing officer. This causes the man to fear not being able to visit his wife for a while. Both he and his wife are angry. They will learn both emotions well in time—"fear and anger."

A man came to me last night in both fear and anger. I was at church with some friends telling dirty jokes. It's quiet there and a welcome change from the cellblocks. This man came and asked me to step outside with him. He wanted to talk. He had just gotten out of the hole for some infraction and seemed upset. When we got outside, he handed me a computer printout. It was the results of the investigation that had been done on him. I read it and handed it back to him. The report said he had been cleared of all charges and was to be released to general population. His anger was at being sent to the hole in the first place, but it was compounded by rumors that he had been hearing about being called a "snitch," because he got out of the hold on such a charge. His fear was the loss of his family visits (trailer visits) and at the man he felt was spreading these rumors—anger and fear.

Stories of anger and fear are all over these places. The helpless feeling one experiences as he watches his family change before his eyes brings anger at his helplessness and fear of what is taking place. He is becoming a stranger to his family. In time, this man will finally learn to accept the fact that he has become a very angry stranger to everyone he once held dear in his life. He will learn to live with fear, and even start to look forward to the same situations that used to cause fear in him: a fist fight, some officer getting knocked on his ass, or a rumor of an evident gang war with weapons. He starts seeking these things out. With time, this man finds that he needs the unsettling feeling of danger and fear to stay alive inside—to keep his mind off the inner deadness and anger he feels.

With danger and fear, he can express his anger; he can once again feel alive. He will become good at generating fear in others. He will become that which he most hated when he came to prison; a mental, physical, or psychological bully. In reality, he does exactly what he sees the system is doing. He becomes judgmental. He thrives on rumor and acts on it. He loses sight of fairness and finds himself getting involved in a negative manner in the lives of others. To cover his own fear and anger, he attempts to force it on others. Of course, he learns to laugh to cover his true inner feelings—to laugh AT fear and IN anger.

At this point, he has an unrecognized addiction to fear. He needs it to cover the deadness he feels inside and uses it as an outlet for his anger. He is now a person society will not tolerate. Life outside prison becomes boring. The average citizen seems stupid in their outlook on life. The very thought being content and happy in a world he once valued so highly, is but a memory. He hates almost everything. He fears almost everything. But most of all, he hates himself for the anger he can't escape.

In time, however, if he doesn't die as a result of this anger and fear, as many around him will, he will seek answers through religion, meditation, and even self-denial. Yes, and he will, if he is lucky, find the person that he buried so long ago under that pile of fear and anger. He will break away from that person that the system created. He will start to remember softness, feel love, and see a different world.

He may start to set goals for himself that would have been beneath him only a few years in the past. He may even understand and attempt to help those around him in any manner possible. He has gone the full circle "taker to giver." Now, he hates fear. He wants no one to experience it as he did. He hates and is easily angered by those addicted to fear as he once was. He is a reformed asshole at worst, and can possibly even laugh at himself for what he has been. The anger and fear he feels now is but a memory. A memory of the old man he sees in the mirror, the gray-haired old man that wasted so much of his life in "anger and fear."

It is said that, "Life can only be understood backwards—but it must be lived forward."

STRANGER BEHIND GLASS

Columbia County Jail: I entered the jail visiting room, found a seat near the wall and picked up the telephone that connected me with my visitor on the other side of a 3/4 inch Plexiglass security shield. The Plexiglass was clouded with age and wear.

The stools both my visitor and I were sitting on were round bare metal and bolted to the floor. In bright coarse orange coveralls three sizes too small and without underwear, I attempted to gain some sort of comfortable position as I looked through the clouded glass.

"How is she going den Eddie?" the old man said, his hand shaking as he held the telephone.

"Aw, it's okay... How are you feeling?" I asked.

"Oh, good as can be 'spected.'"

I take note of his hands. They are little but skincovered bones. Not the big powerful hands of the rancher, farmer and garbage collector he had been in days past. He seemed smaller somehow. His hair gray, his eyes bloodshot from the medication he was forced to take; even his voice seemed to shake.

"Did you have to wait long before they let you in?" I ask.

"Naw, yust had a cop o' coffee and da ettagarrren guard (crazy guard), let me right in," he tells me in his English/

Norwegian mixture I knew so well.

"I got something to show you now, Eddie," he says as he brings an old metal box out of a paper bag. Carefully he opens the box. I can see that the box itself is antique hand-painted metal. His eyes brighten with pride as he picks out a gold plated railroad watch with a long chain.

"Bet ya never saw one like dis one before," he tells me as he tries to untangle the chain from the remaining treasures, in the box with his free hand. Finally, with shaky hands, he lays the phone down and separates the contents of his box.

"Yep, dey yust don't make 'em like dis anymore; look here at dis one too," he continues as he digs out several old wrist watches, some old gold, rings and several dozen old coins.

He shows each piece to me proudly; they are his secret treasure. He has found every one of them in the garbage over the last twenty five years. Each item has a little story, when and where he found them and how lucky he was to have always looked into the garbage real good.

"Yep, one never knows what one will find."

I'm sad, I see the face of a dying stranger, my father.

I lie to him,

"Well, I think you are looking better now."

"Oh ya, some days it's better den udders, you know," he says trying to make light of what we both know.

"Dey tell me dat you will be leaving to go to dat prison in da morning, so I just tot I better get down to see you before you go. Never know what can happen des days ya know. Yep, you Just lissen to me now Eddie, just in case somting happens before you get out of dat prison. I want you to go see your sister Sandra; she knows."

"It's about da house an stuff, ya know. I already took care o' everting and Sandra knows what to do. I don't tink I'll be able to get all da way down to dat prison to see ya, so it's better we talk now," he says with his hands shaking and tears in his eyes.

My heart is breaking. He knows that death is just around the corner. I can see it too. We both know this will be the last time we'll see each other. A dying father speaking to his only son. Two fractured hearts attempting to communicate. Two grown men who love each other dearly, attempting to face a final goodbye. He fingers those treasures before him, behind the clouded glass, as we sneak fleeting looks at each other, careful not to make eye contact. We are both afraid to face the other, for fear of tears, and the denial of what's happening.

So many times over the years I had seen the guilt in his eyes, guilt for the beatings he gave me as a child. So many times I wanted to tell him that it was okay; it was over, and that it wasn't his fault. But I never did. I didn't know how. As time passed, my going to prison created guilt on my part. Now we sit, made strangers by guilt, bound by blood and love, strangers through violence and guilt.

I wanted to say, "Dad, I'm sorry your only son turned out to be a family outcast, the only member of your family ever convicted of committing a crime. I'm sorry for the pain and shame I've caused you."

I'm sure he would have liked to say,

"Eddie, I should never have beat you like I did when you were just a little one."

But, we said nothing, we were strangers to expressing feelings. We didn't know how.

"Your twenty minutes are up." The guard said.

"Well, guess I better be going now, Eddie you just take care o' yourself now."

"I'll be okay, Don't worry about me, Dad," I said, watching his aged, shaking hands gather up his treasures.

The tears come; I can hide them no longer. When he looks up, he too has tears streaming down both cheeks. Finally we both are forced to look directly at each other. We both can see the pain in the other. Then in a shaking voice he says,

"Good bye, Eddie; you take care now."

"Bye, Dad."

I watch this old man through the clouded Plexiglas as he turns and slowly leaves the visiting room, in tears, bent with age and speechless in pain. I feel anger at myself for not taking the time to know this stranger better; this stranger that I love so much.

Why didn't we go camping just once? Why didn't I at least try to lift the guilt he carries? Why hadn't we ever learned to talk like the men we were, father and son? Now it's too late; he is dying and all I can do is watch him leave through the clouded glass. It's over; there are no more chances; time has run out for us.

"Good bye, Eddie."

"Good bye, Dad."

Strangers who finally ran out of time.=

* My father died several months later while I was in prison. I didn't get to attend his funeral, so we were both right. The last time we would see each other was through that

clouded Plexiglass, in that county jail visiting room, strangers to the bitter end.

Guess the only truly honest emotion we ever shared was in that visiting room. That clouded Plexiglass separating my father and me was in reality no more a barrier than the guilt we both carried over so many years. The Plexiglass I could touch with my hand; the guilt I could only touch with my heart.

EDDIE OR DUKE?

I used to be a pretty good businessman, looked good in a suit, could hold a crowd's attention when speaking and was thought to be intelligent by some people. Went to Emanuel Lutheran Church, drove a new pickup, lived in a nice new split-level home, had a pretty wife and three little boys who called me Daddy. My family included a Professor at Kentucky State University, a Medical Doctor who headed up a hospital surgical department in North Dakota and two sisters Judy and Sandra, who depended on me for almost everything.

I used to be a lot of things. Today I'm supposed to be a rehabilitated convict. My little boys have grown up and have families of their own, my pretty young wife has remarried another man, and my sisters no longer even take the time to write me. In fact, I'm a stranger to all who used to call me Eddie, including myself.

I'm called Duke in prison today. Memories flash through my mind like a horrible technicolor strobe light. Flashes of wrestling with my little boys, interrupted by memories of fighting the prison riot squads, to softly kissing and making love to my pretty wife, to stumbling stripped-naked through a gauntlet of prison guards with the burn of pepper spray blinding me, and feeling the blows from night sticks, to remembering every gentle tinkling syllable of a child's tiny voice, to the screaming violent threat of bullet and bull horns. From the pride I remember in the family I had, to the shame I feel for the pain I've caused them. To the surging rage I felt as I attacked an armed horse-mounted prison guard—to the recollections of my little Daughter, in pigtails, feeding me popcorn one piece at a time and calling me Bombee. Truly, a roller-coaster of life's reminiscences, constantly flashing on the screen of my mind.

I now question if there is a middle ground to my life's remembrances. Is it possible for the businessman, Father, dependable Brother, and Church Member, once known as Eddie, to ever look at life in the same open trusting way? Was too much of Eddie lost or crippled, so Duke could survive in prison? Does life offer a common denominator into which both Eddie and Duke will fit? And who am I this second— **EDDIE OR DUKE?**

BUDDY BEARS

A young man approached me bashfully on the yard the other day. He had a legal question. His clothes were clean and neat, but seemed much too large for his frame. His hat was on sideways too. His dress told me he was a gang member; his eyes told me he was a kid, bashfully asking a question.

"Hey Duke, some guys told me you know about law," he said.

"They lied," I answered.

He then kind of chuckled and asked if I minded if he asked me a few questions.

"Go for it," I told him.

"My attorney hasn't answered my letters and won't take a collect call from me. Hell man, I don't know what's happening with my appeal or nothing. What should I do?"

"Your attorney Court appointed?" I asked.

"Yes, does that make a difference?"

"All the difference in the world. I'll tell you what though, the short answer to your question is to write the Court of Appeals and tell them exactly what you told me. They will remind your attorney to stay in contact with you."

"Aright! Hey man, thanks," he said turning to leave.

"Hold up there a second, I'll make you a deal. You and a couple of your buddies answer a few questions for me and

I'll even type that letter to the Court of Appeals for you," I said.

"What you wanna know?"

"Well, for starters, who in hell taught you to wear a hat," I said laughing. He laughed, too, and said it was the "in" thing.

"I just want to talk to some gang bangers and find out what makes you little farts tick," I told him.

"Okay; that's cool Duke. Do ya wanna talk to some of the home boys right now?"

"May as well, damn sure ain't nothin' else to do."

With that the youngster said he would be right back and headed over to a group he hung out with. I watched as he talked to them and pointed in my direction. Finally four of his "Home Boys," got up and approached me. My first impression was kids, that's all they were, just kids.

"Old Duke wants to know how come we wear our caps sideways," said the young man. Everyone got a good, but nervous laugh out of it. Two of the gang bangers even straightened their hats out, laughing.

"How many guys in your gang?" I asked. They all kinda laughed and told me about "Turf" and the "Hood" (neighborhood), explaining that the size of a gang depended on the area they lived in. Overall, they seemed secure in their belief that "Gangs" were the only way to survive in the "Hoods" they lived in.

One of them mentioned something about "Buddy Bears" and everyone started laughing.

"What's a Buddy Bear," I asked.

"It's a little stuffed bear the cops give you after they come into your house and beat the hell out of your dad and haul him off to jail."

"Everybody gets them," one of the kids said.

"They kicked the door down at my place once, slammed my mom on the floor, and took my old man and pushed his face so hard into the wall that his face got cut on the thermostat, handcuffed him and hauled him off to jail."

"Then this lady cop comes in and gives me and my sisters some Buddy Bears, so we wouldn't feel bad. Every time I looked at that bear, I thought about my old man's blood on the wall by that thermostat. Even my little sisters hated those damn Buddy Bears."

"How many of you guys got Buddy Bears," I asked.

They all got a good laugh out of that and said, "Everybody got at least one of those damn things. It's the reward you get for watching your family beat up in the projects. Sometimes they give them to you when the child welfare workers come to take you to some foster home, too. You know, take ya away from your family and put ya up with some strangers. Hell, I used to hide my marijuana in mine, case workers never looked there for my weed." That brought another round of laughter from the kids.

" So, you feel safer in gangs, is that right?" I asked.

"Hell yes, those pigs don't be handin' me no buddy bears these days. When they come kickin' in doors now days in the hood, they better be wearing bullet proof everything. I hear that an old deer rifle will go right through one of those bullet proof vests, too," said another kid.

After listening to them discuss the types of guns needed to penetrate bullet proof vests for a while, I got an uneasy feeling. Those kids seemed set on nothing but destruction or revenge. Taking whatever they could from anyone they could. They called it "payback,"

They knew the names of the best neighborhoods in all the surrounding areas. They talked of "Popping Caps" (shooting), into groups of citizens, of taking pot shots at cops traveling through the neighborhoods. No talk about making a score or doing a crime for money. They didn't speak about drugs or alcohol. They were turned on by "payback."

"What happens when you shoot into a crowd, and the next morning you read in the paper that you crippled a 34 year old mother with four kids—like what happened in Tacoma last year. Wouldn't you feel guilty?" I asked.

Again, they laughed. Then one of them said.,

"Hell, give her a Buddy Bear; that's what they gave us. They got nothin' comin'. Citizens even watch on television how cops come into the projects and beat people, an' they laugh. Way I see it, if ya saw it on television an' didn't do nothin' 'bout it, you as guilty as the cops what done it.

I hate 'em all. Cops an' those "do good" citizens who see what is happenin' an I don't do nothin' 'bout it. Cops just for the rich peoples, 'ats all. Like I say, they got nothin' comin'. It's our turn now an' we gonna get ours; ya can believe that."

Guess I got one hell of a lesson. Those kids are not like any convict I ever met. I could actually feel the anger in them. I knew it wasn't the Buddy Bears, that was just an excuse. I also knew these kids were very dangerous. Angry kids, with guns, whose goal was payback. If you weren't from their "Hood," you were the enemy.

With that I shook my head and brought the question and answer session to a close. They played with the angle of their caps for a minute or two and laughed.

"You a writer on the streets, Duke?" one asked.

"Hell no," I said, " I'm a wino!"

They all cracked up at that remark and one of them said Winos were cool. Guess that made me feel a little better, knowing these kids were not hunting winos. I'll tell you what, though; these kids aren't governed by greed or an easy buck. They are motivated by the blood on that thermostat, and the society that allowed it to happen.

Scary, ain't it? How a soft little bear, meant to do good, can be a reminder of a nightmare and invoke so much hatred. I know that the police officer who gives children a bear, does so out of kindness. Guess I'm confused as to how something given with love can be so wrongly received. Wrong place, wrong time and wrong reminder, I guess.

We have a whole generation whose abuse and neglect was purchased with a **BUDDY BEAR.**

ABUSE AND NEGLECT

There are so many kinds of abuse that I can't begin to address them here. I was physically and mentally abused as a child. It's impossible to physically abuse anyone without mentally abusing them also. This abuse resulted in me being ignorant of the basic tools needed to maintain and enjoy a long term relationship. It took me decades to truly trust anyone.

My father was raised in a very cold and physical atmosphere. His values were to support a family and see that we had food and clothing, first and foremost. He didn't know how to express softness and love in any other manner. His generation seldom expressed feeling. They were God-fearing, hardworking and self-supporting. They were mentally tough and limited in the emotional skills we so openly demonstrate today. It isn't that he didn't want to or that he didn't know what should be done; he just didn't know how to do it.

I have no doubt that my father loved me dearly. Now, for him to tell me that face to face, well, it would be impossible for him, or at the very least, terribly embarrassing. Thus, I didn't know how to express emotion or feeling until well into my teens. Even then it was an act for me, I often didn't feel what I was saying. My true feelings were well hidden. It isn't that I didn't want to. I knew what should have been done; I just didn't know how to do it.

The single most obvious result of the abuse I took as a child has made it impossible for me to ever even spank a child. I can't stand to be in the same room when a child is being spanked, either. It's something about the fear in a child's eyes. It wasn't until I was in my late thirties that I could look one of my children in the eye and tell them I loved them, I was proud of them, and I was sorry for not being there when they needed me the most. And, I'm still not good at it.

Oh, the feeling is there, but the know-how isn't. It's taken me a long time to learn to be soft, to not cover the feelings I have. It becomes easier to say I love you, each time I do it, however, and I am learning.

Today, when I see a young man come into prison acting tough, I feel like puking. The vast majority of people in prison today are God-fearing, mixed-up addicts of some type. I've yet to meet an atheist in prison. I've yet to meet that flat-nosed humanoid, without a conscience, also.

Believe me, I searched for him for years too. I believed he was in every prison in America, had to be. I had seen him on television, heard about him on the news and had been told of him by cops. He is only a figment of the imagination, a mirage, used to convince an un-knowing public of the need for more and bigger prisons.

The prison industry flourishes. It's one of the biggest career opportunities going these days. It is also one of this country's biggest failures. Prisons teach lonely, mixed-up, addicts and misfits to hate; that's all—pure and simple. Then, after that has been done, they give the prisoner forty dollars and turn him loose on society.

So many times I've seen news cameras come into a prison for one thing or another. They are very careful who they interview. They try hard to project, on camera, the stereotyped image of a convict. Lots of tattoos, a flat nose with a poor command of English; the person everyone has been warned about for decades. They seldom show the young scared kid, the old typical grandfather or the college professor. When was the last time a television program filmed a bunch of prisoners on their knees in prayer?

In the last story in this book, "Sunray Catcher," I make the statement, "On his knees, in a 'very convict like' manner." That is because there are more prisoners by far on their knees than there are running around killing and raping without a conscience, as the media would have you believe.

There are many types of abuse exercised in every prison in America today. In some cases, the abuse by officials even carries over to the prisoner's family. We should be used to it, some 80% of us were abused in some manner as children. Perhaps abuse corrects abuse, in the minds of corrections officials.

There are many people in corrections who really want to make a difference, good and caring people. They want to make change, but like my father and me they just don't know quite how to do it.

Somewhere, at sometime, a wise man will step forward and explain to one and all, that in fact, **ABUSE AND NEGLECT,** of any type, no matter when or where it is, is the real father of most wrongs.

FUZZY

Most of the stories I write are about convicts. However, I've also met many corrections officials who were kind and caring people. The following story is about one such officer I'll call "Fuzzy."

Fuzzy was a beautiful young lady with long curly hair. She was married and going to college while working at Oregon State Penitentiary several years ago. Fuzzy was one of those people who just made you smile meeting her. She had the ability to disarm the toughest old cons with humor and seemed to make us want to protect her. Besides, she always smelled good. Today, I don't know where she is or what she is doing, so I'll have to only use the name Fuzzy for her. However, if she reads this, I hope she forgives me for telling the following story.

After the evening meal in the prison chow hall, my friend Mac McGuire and myself were walking to the cell block area. I lit a cigarette and Mac got on me about it.

"Duke, ya gotta quit smoking. Those things are gonna kill ya!," he said. I'd heard the same lecture from Mac many times over the years.

Mac was a real health fanatic. He lifted weights and had the body to prove it. He also ate vitamins by the handful and even ate wheat germ—and, of course, constantly complained about me smoking.

My answer to Mac was always the same too.

"I know it Mac, just shut up, you're worse than my ex-wife."

Mac would laugh, punch me in the shoulder and we would do it again next time.

This night, Mac told me his neck was bothering him. He thought he might have pulled a muscle lifting weights. After I finished my cigarette, we went our separate ways—Mac to his assigned cell block and me to mine.

A few hours later, a very excited watch commander rushed into my cell asking for a phone number for Mac's family. He explained that they had found Mac on the floor in his cell, dead of an apparent heart attack.

I asked the watch commander if I could go and see my friend one last time and was told it was okay with him, as long as it was okay with the medical people.

Walking into D-block seemed strange. Five tiers high and 40 cells long, it was normally noisy to the point of a roar. Now, however, it seemed almost spooky quiet. The wing sergeant told me the medical people were done with Mac's body and that it was locked in the cage at the rear of the cell block.

As I walked down the long quiet tier, I stopped at my old friend Curly"s cell. Curly was sitting on his bunk, in silence with tears in his eyes. He moved his finger up to his lips and motioned for me to be quiet—to listen. I stood there for a few seconds, then quietly continued on. I could hear singing from the cage at the rear of the cell block—muffled singing—someone trying hard not to be heard. It was a religious song—"Amazing Grace."

When I got up to the cage, I could see my friend's body on a stretcher and over in the corner, singing in hushed tones, was Fuzzy—singing as she stood guard over my friend's body.

Guess I stood there for a few seconds, said the convict's prayer, and left quietly. When I passed Curly's cell on my way out, he whispered,

"Fuzzy?"

I nodded my head and we both just looked at the floor. I don't know if we were saddest over what death had done to our friend Mac or what death was doing to Fuzzy.

Note: Hopefully today **FUZZY** is a soccer mom and her husband, a coach, in some West Coast high school. Guys like Curly and me can't deal with Fuzzy's pain very well.

FROM A CRYING FATHER

I was talking to my publisher on the phone last night, when she asked me if I minded talking to a good friend of hers, a Minister from the area in Washington State where I had lived at one time. Course, the first thing that hit me was, I'm not real good at talking to Ministers. I'm too plain spoken—to put it mildly. Whatever, I agreed to talk to her friend.

When Bob came on the line, his voice was clear and friendly,

"Hi there, Duke."

We talked a bit about men we both knew in the area, about his thirty five years working on the waterfront, and a newspaper he wanted me to read.

"This paper really tells it like it is," he told me.

"The publishers have been subject to many kinds of pressure to curb their writings, but they have persevered. I have read some of your writings, and I had to quit reading at times; they sure got to me."

Then in a raspy, choked voice, he said,

"My son is in prison, you know."

A few seconds of silence followed.

"They sentenced him to over a hundred months. The State Supreme Court overturned part of his sentence, but he still shouldn't be in there."

Silence again for a few seconds. Sadly, men cry different from women; we hide our emotions. Here was a father
desperately seeking an answer to what he knew was totally
wrong. A part of him, his son, had been unfairly sent to
prison. This man was no wimp. He had worked with his
hands on the waterfront for over thirty five years. I could feel
the pain in his voice when he said,

"I'll spend every dime I have, to get my boy justice."

I could feel what this man was saying. He's willing to
spend everything he has worked for, everything he has saved
to get justice for his son, without question. His heart was broken, and he didn't know what to do or where to turn. He was
fighting the monster that took his son from him with everything he had.

"I was wondering if you would mind if I sent in a few
of your stories to that newspaper, Duke?" he asked.

"I cried when I read them. Other people need to see
your writings and find out just how corrupt the system has
become."

I told him to feel free to do whatever he wanted with
my writings. I could tell him the name of an attorney I knew,
who wasn't afraid to fight the system. What do you tell a man
of God, who finds out what he always believed to be honest
and fair is mired in corruption and greed, to the point they
openly flaunt their dishonesty in everyone's face?

Like "The Crying Mother," I couldn't tell him the truth.
I could only offer hope with the name of an attorney.

Then he told me,

"When you get out, if you have no one to come and
get you, I'll be glad to do it. You can stay at my place until
your publisher comes to get you ... My home is yours."

About that time, the phone line went dead. It seems to happen often when the conversation on the line is about a corrupt system. I tried to call back several times, but the line was dead.

Yes, I'll meet this **"CRYING FATHER"** one day. We may go for a walk and talk about the newspaper. Two crying fathers, men from opposite spectrums of life, men who have lost parts of their lives to a monster called prison. Two wounded men fighting the same foe, a Minister of God and a tough old convict, brought together by tears and pain. Tonight, I'll pray for Bob's son and tomorrow I'll wake to fight this monster again, stronger now, because a Minister from Kalama Washington, stands with me.

"A MOTHER'S LOVE "

She came to visit her son Roger every week. She was one of those plump little women who seem ageless. Her hair was graying, tied back tightly in a bun. Her clothes worn, but clean, and she had a perpetual smile on her face. As far as I can remember, I have never seen her without a coat of some type on. She seemed to always be holding her coat tightly in front. Her face was very expressive and she often ended her sentences with "You know." She called me Norski, with a giggle, and I called her Swede.

One day I was waiting for a visit from my youngest son when she came in. She was dressed in a bright pink and blue windbreaker. When she sat down, I said,

"Nice jacket there, Swede."

She visibly blushed and adjusted her jacket saying thank you to me. When her son and mine hadn't shown up, she moved over to the chair next to mine.

"I got such a buy on this coat, you know," she said. "I only paid four dollars for it, you know. A person can get some real bargains if one watches real close, you know. You can't even tell it's used now, can you?"

"No, I sure can't," I told her.

"My boy Roger, he was so good to me before he went to prison, you know," she went on. He once bought me a lit-

144

tle bottle of perfume that cost over twenty dollars, you know," she said, her voice in a conspiratorial whisper.

"I never would wear something that expensive when I go shopping at the Goodwill Store, you know. I keep it in a nice safe place."

Her eyes had a mischievous sparkle as she told me of her hidden expensive perfume. Then I told her that she was really a big help to her son Roger, by coming to visit him so regularly every week.

Oh, it's nothing. I can come all the way here on the bus for only five dollars and thirty cents you know. I can go here and back again for only eight and a half dollars, too. It's cheaper that way you know, when you buy the ticket to go both ways from the start."

Then, in a very secretive voice, after she looked around to make sure that no one was listening to us, she said,

"I can leave my Roger five dollars from time to time too you know. Yes, I got myself a real money maker, I'll tell you. Now, you can't breath a word of this."

When I agreed with a nod, she whispered again,

"I go to the blood plasma place and donate every week, you know. That gives me fifteen dollars so I can get down here to see my Roger, but you will never guess what else I'm doing. I've been going to the other plasma center and donating once a week too. I just spell my name a little different and there it is, another fifteen dollars, you know."

"Well, that's quite a trick," I told her, "but isn't that dangerous for you to do that two times every week?"

"Oh, I'm healthy as a horse, you know. I got this coat for four dollars and I can leave my Roger five dollars too, you know. He is just a little boy really, and you know how those kids like a candy bar once in a while," she said with a proud sparkle in her eye.

I don't ever want anyone to talk to me about **A MOTH-ER'S LOVE.** That four dollar pink and blue windbreaker, covered the most unselfish and unconditional loving heart I've ever seen. So often it happens that way for the families of prisoners. The family suffers and does time right along with the prisoner. The rich seldom go to prison and the poor get by as best they can.

OLD YELLOW HAT

This old yellow hat... Seems it's become part of my identity. A friend asked me the other day why I hadn't been to the yard the prior evening. He had been looking for someone tall with a yellow hat on the prison yard. I had left the hat in my cell that night; consequently, he had overlooked me in the crowd.

When I arrived here from Washington State Penitentiary in Walla Walla, this hat was given to me by Jim Thorne. I didn't know Jim well at the time. He just seemed to blend quietly in the background, near some of the men I did know. He was tall, thin, had very expressive eyes, and a ready smile. One of the first things I noticed about Jim was his hearty laugh. He laughed out loud anytime, anywhere. It came as a total surprise to me when Jim asked me bashfully if I wanted this hat. Several days later, I noticed Jim wearing an old beat-up hat. The hat he had given me was his best one, the only new hat he owned.

Over the next couple months, I got to know Jim better. I found that there was a very special person buried in him, buried by years of uncertainty and abuse. Jim had been homeless on the streets. He had lived in missions all across the country and had been deemed 100% mentally disabled by the state. His self-respect was at rock bottom, and he was sentenced to prison for the remainder of his natural life. When I asked Jim if he had killed someone, he said,

"No, I didn't even have a real gun, it was a squirt gun."

He went on to tell me that he had once given some guy a black eye, but had never hurt anyone else. Jim had robbed a hospital gift shop, with a squirt gun. He is a "three strikes you are out" inmate.

The table a convict sits at in the chow hall is a guarded possession. Many fights have taken place over a man's seat in prison chow halls all across America. My seat was offered to me the day I got here. Some old friends from years back invited me to share their table. You are judged by the people you eat with in prison, at least by the other convicts. After I had been here about a month, Jim, again bashfully, asked me if I would like to eat at his table. I did and do.

When writing class opened, I was surprised and happy to hear Jim say he was going to take the class with us. A week or two into the class, Jim even started talking and taking an active part in class. He told me he felt good going to class because someone always saved him a seat if he was late, and the teacher didn't get on him if he didn't have his homework done.

He said he felt safe in class too, because no one ever made fun of him in there. He didn't think he could write anything just yet, but he sure liked being there because everyone had fun.

Well, here it is two and half months later and I still eat at Jim's table, proudly I might add. Now two other very popular and respected convicts eat there too, from time to time, when there is room. My friend Jim is now a tier porter, on the tier where my cell is located, so he stops every morning as he sweeps and mops the tier, to talk and make sure I'm okay.

Today, he told me that he might write a story for our class. He sounded a bit unsure, but he's gonna try. He feels safe in trying to write now. You see, Jim got to pull a good joke on the teacher the other day, a good one, too, he says. He has been bragging about it all week.

"I never got to pull one on somebody as smart as a teacher before, ya know," Jim says proudly.

I bet it's going to be a hell of a story Jim writes too. For a fact, he has paid his dues, being called stupid and crazy most of his life. Jim asks lots of questions, he's still unsure of himself.

"Did I sound dumb in class today, Duke?"

"What do ya think Duke, will I look stupid if I try?"

Yes, lots of questions. However, I've noticed that some of the strongest and most respected convicts in the place always seem to find time to talk to Jim or tease him a little. I hope these men know they are Jim's heros ... I believe they do.

I found out that Jim is a good typist, too. He even graduated from the vocational welding school here in prison and he has a good solid knowledge of the mechanics and punctuation in writing. He often helps teach other inmates in basic math, reading and writing, in his spare time. Jim told me this morning that one of the first things he wants to do if he ever gets out of prison is... Pet a dog.

So, if you ever see me without this hat, it's only because I forgot to put it on, and that's damn seldom. I'm proud of this old yellow hat. Got it from a special kind of friend; yup, real proud of it.

My writing instructor once asked me why a typewriter in my cell would be better than using a computer in the computer lab. I think I told him of how hard it was to get the use of a printer, with thirty students and only four printers. That's true and I've got to admit, it's a wondrous place for someone like me, with good instructors and the input of up to thirty students. Just the idea of being able to see everything, and spellcheck it before printing, is pure magic to me.

If I could write stories of clean, just, and always rose-colored things in real life, there would be no better place for me, but I don't and can't. I could write a real gut-twister story about my friend Jim Thorne and the injustice in his life, but not in a computer lab. I would have to do it in my cell, alone and in private. You see, I cry sometimes when writing about things really important to me. I can't do that in the wonderful magic place of computers with thirty people watching.

I guess it's all in how a person looks at things really. Some people see everything in life as nice, clean and just. I envy them and their world of beauty and perfect justice. Guess I see things different sometimes. Just take this **OLD YELLOW HAT** for instance, the one my friend Jim gave me. When I look at it... It ain't yellow ... This hat is gold, if I ever saw it.

NURSE BONNIE

As far as I know, everyone just called her Bonnie. I can't recall her last name today. However, she was truly one in a million. About 1971, Bonnie was a nurse on the second floor of the prison hospital at Washington State Penitentiary in Walla Walla, Washington. She was one of those "hands-on people."

Whenever Bonnie talked to a person, she seemed to have her hand on that person's arm hand or was trying to straighten the person's collar or something. She seemed to always have time to talk to everyone and—let me tell you—she could talk! Yak, yak yak! But, we all loved her and it was evident that she truly cared for us.

At that time there was a big convict named Elmer Hardy, also doing time. Elmer, had been shot in the forehead with a .38 caliber pistol by a Seattle police officer. The bullet split when it hit Elmer and thus didn't kill him. It did, however, retard him to about the mentality of an eight year old child.

Elmer, was a big, black, giant of a man. The bullet caused such damage to Elmer's brain that he forgot how to read and write—plus it caused him terrible headaches, when he failed to take his medication. These headaches put Elmer into violent screaming rages.

When this happened, the goon squad (special guards trained in hand-to-hand fighting) was called and they took him to the hospital for his shot. The cost was high however.

The one thing Elmer never did forget, was how to fight. He would put several of those specially trained guards on medical leave, every time they tried to subdue him.

I was working in the prison hospital at the time. One day Bonnie came to my work area leading a bashful Elmer by the hand.

"Duke, have you met my friend Elmer?" she asked.

I knew enough about Elmer Hardy to stay the hell away from him. As far as that goes, it was a well-known fact that there wasn't any two convicts in the whole place that could take the black giant in a fist fight. But I said, "Yes, I knew him," and hoped it would end there. He just plain scared me. It seemed most everyone was afraid of Elmer—except Bonnie, that is.

"Well," she said with a wink, "Elmer has a problem. He lost his reading glasses so he can't read or write very good. He has a letter from his daughter that he has been carrying around for over a month and he's too bashful to ask anyone to read it for him. I want you to read it to him and help him answer it if he wants to. Will you do that for me, Duke?"

What could I say? The poor guy was ashamed of not being able to read and he had been carrying that letter around all this time, so I read the letter to the big bashful man-child.

It was from his only daughter. Seems she just had a child and wanted to know if Elmer, wanted some pictures of the baby. She hadn't seen Elmer in over twelve years. She also wanted her father to arrange things so she could come and visit him. When I finished reading the letter to Elmer, Bonnie made a big fuss over it.

"Elmer, you are a Grandpa! Do you know that Elmer, YOU are a real GRANDPA! Yak, yak, Yak!

Elmer smiled bashfully, his enormous head wobbling side to side. The scene was truly one for the books. Here was this tiny, uniformed white prison nurse, bouncing around this big, very dangerous, unpredictable black convict—so happy—she was just vibrating and pinching the black giant's cheek as she teased him about being a Grandpa.

After a while, Bonnie finally calmed down and left so Elmer and I could answer the letter. Elmer said in a deep halting voice,

"Maybe ya can read it 'gain ta me, 'cause I don't hear so good neither."

So I read it again, and again, and again. After each reading Elmer would ask a few questions.

"How do tha baby know I'm his Grandpa?"

"Do tha baby like me? "

"How do tha baby know me?

Finally, after countless readings and questions, Elmer and I got the letter answered. We sent a visiting form with it too. In the weeks that followed, Elmer would bring any new letter he got to Bonnie, who would in turn bring him back to my work area and the whole process would start all over again.

Soon, I found myself looking forward to helping Elmer with his letters. I also found the gentleness in him that Bonnie had so quickly discovered.

One day, when Elmer and I were working on one of his letters, Bonnie came in and sat down. After listening and watching us for a few minutes, she asked,

"Elmer, if you could have anything you wanted in here, what would it be? "

"Oh, nottin'" Elmer answered bashfully, "I'm okay."

There must be something you would want in here Elmer," Bonnie persisted,

"Now you think about it and then let Duke know three things that would make you happy in here, Elmer."

A few days later, Elmer came up to me on the prison yard. He told me that if he could have anything he wanted, it would be to watch cartoons on television in the mornings, have a prison job like the other convicts and to have Tootsie Rolls. I, in turn, relayed Elmer's wishes to Bonnie.

To make a long story short, Bonnie went to the watch commander and talked him into giving Elmer the job of cleaning the television rooms on weekends, thus he would be alone to watch his cartoons and have a job too. That took care of two of his wishes. The Tootsie Rolls weren't sold at the inmate store, so Bonnie would bring him in 4 or 5 of those little penny Tootsie Rolls every day she worked.

Elmer did an excellent job cleaning those television rooms. He even had his own Ajax, mop, bucket and rags, locked in a special janitor's closet. He was proud of all "his stuff," as he called it. And, of course, any convict with an ounce of brains wouldn't even dream of messing up Elmer's television rooms. You would be surprised how clean and considerate those convicts were when they knew they had to answer to Elmer for any mess they left.

Bonnie and I noticed something else. Whenever either of us had to go anywhere in the prison, Elmer wasn't far behind. We were both teased by others who couldn't help but notice that we had a full-time bodyguard. Elmer was making sure that no one messed with his Tootsie Roll connection. He would also meet Bonnie at the front gate every day when she came to work, faithfully, so he could get those treasured Tootsie Rolls.

One day Bonnie heard on the guard's radio, that Elmer was going wild with a headache again in four wing. The goon squad was called and the hospital alerted, to expect Elmer and possibly some injured guards. The side door of the hospital was right off a long walkway known as "Blood Alley," due to the of amount killings that had happened there.

Only on rare occasions would a guard walk down Blood Alley by himself. At the end of Blood Alley, maybe 200 feet, was the door to four wing where Elmer lived. Bonnie—alone—ran to four wing, ahead of the goon squad to confront Elmer. She walked up to the front of his cell with a stern look on her face and scolded the raving giant, much like a person might scold an eight year old child.

"Elmer! Now you just quit this and come over to the hospital with me right now! This is foolish, Elmer, and if you don't settle down right now, I'm never going to get you another Tootsie Roll again, yak, yak, yak!"

Man! Bonnie sure laid into Elmer. By the time the goon squad reached four wing, Bonnie and her Tootsie Roll bodyguard, were already walking out, on their way to the hospital. Elmer was following a constantly yakking Bonnie, rubbing his aching head and agreeing with every word she said in defense of those Tootsie Rolls.

Twenty four years later, I again came through Washington State Penitentiary. Elmer had died in the late 1970s, the delayed result of that bullet wound. Bonnie however, was there, ready to retire and for the most part, unchanged. She told me that her husband had died several years before, her daughters were now grown with families of their own and she was still a Christian. We talked about the old days for about fifteen minutes and when it came time for me to go, I asked her,

"Have you run into any more Tootsie Roll bodyguards Bonnie? "

For possibly the first time in all the years that I've have known her, Bonnie was completely quiet for a few moments, just staring out the prison hospital window. Then with tears in her eyes she turned to face me and said,

"Wasn't he a little sweetheart?"

Yes, to Bonnie, the black giant was a little sweetheart. I guess anyone who is hurt or handicapped, even us convicts, are sweethearts to Elmer Hardy's Tootsie Roll connection, **NURSE BONNIE.**

THINGS IMPORTANT

Working in a prison hospital emergency room, I've seen the unscheduled execution all too often.—men who ate in the same chow hall with me just a couple hours before entering the emergency room with a shocked, surprised look on their faces. Some angry, but mostly crying, and asking why...

"My God, why did he stab me? I was gonna pay him," or, "I wasn't the one that called him a snitch."

Later, a type of calm comes over the person. Maybe it's acceptance. They remember things that were not important until death was taking away any chance of ever doing them.

"My wife always wanted to go camping with me. God, this can't really be happening. Please God, don't let this happen. How could I be so stupid? I wonder if my kid made the baseball team, ya know I've only seen the little fart play two times, was always too busy getting loaded. Now, it's over, I'll never get the chance to go camping or watch the kid play ball. All over some bullshit! Oh God!"

I've stood there helpless, angry at death, angry with the man dying for his too late recognition of what's really important in life. Angry that a life can be lost over a word, rumor or an unpaid bill. Angry that some little baseball player would be deprived of his real Daddy just because his Daddy was stupid or careless. Mad as hell at a system that causes such things to happen and the "could-care-less" way they look at the killing of an inmate.

I was in Arlington, Texas one time. Went into a little all night market to buy some beer. After I paid the clerk and started to leave, I remembered that I also needed some cigarettes. Turning to ask for the forgotten cigarettes, I noticed the next man in line was already being waited on, so I stood silently waiting. When the clerk looked at me, I told her that I forgot to get cigarettes. She just smiled and said she would be with me in just a second. The next man in line, however, said, "You had your turn... Ya should go to the end of the line if ya can't even remember what ya wanted..."

The clerk and the other man in line seemed kinda embarrassed. The clerk said something like, "It's okay; it will only take a second." But, I was unsure of what to do because I had just been released from T.D.C. (Texas Dept. of Corrections). So, I said it was okay and started to go around again.

The only other person in line, an older man said, "Don't be silly. Get your cigarettes; I'm in no hurry," and kinda gave the man doing the talking a dirty look. So, I stood there and waited. The feeling I had was of being unsure. I didn't want to be impolite and didn't want to upset anyone. But, I couldn't figure out why the man behind me was so openly negative, like he was ordering me to the end of the line. The negative man now asked the clerk if he could cash a check. She said it was okay if he had three pieces of ID. With that, this man started throwing his driver's license, some credit card, and another card out on the counter, appearing angry. I was uncomfortable as I didn't know if he was upset about me or just didn't like the idea of having to show ID. The clerk picked up one of the pieces of ID and looked at it carefully. She then asked the man what "T.D.C." was. "I'm a sergeant at the prison in Longview, Texas," he said.

At that point, everything made perfect sense. I hit him with a damn good straight overhand right, just below the jaw hinge, and heard his jaw snap like a 22 shot. I heard him snort and saw him hit the floor. He was out only a few seconds and then sat up wiping the blood off his mouth with the the back of his hand.

He didn't look puzzled. He didn't even ask why. He knew. At that second, that bastard knew that I was a convict, one of the men he had been abusing for years; one of the nightmares he had on a regular basis. He had no questions. He knew why his jaw was broken.

However, he didn't know what I knew. Ya see, he was much more than a prison guard to me, more even than the sadistic, uncaring bastard he had become. To me, he was the ANSWER TO MANY PRAYERS. Prayers that I had said over the bodies of young dead inmates while listening to the laughter of the guards in the background. Prayers I said after listening to my wife tell of remarks made by guards to her. And prayers said alone, at night in my cell, facing the wall, after having been wronged in some manner by the unaccountable, uncaring actions of a guard. Even prayers said for little baseball players with stupid Daddys.

Too bad I couldn't follow that bastard to whatever emergency room he was headed for, just to laugh in the background. Nope, I just got my cigarettes and walked out, happy and uncaring as any prison guard ya ever saw. THANK YA LORD!!

FROM LEFT TO RIGHT, MY SONS:
KENT, GUY (HOLDING OUR DOG PORKCHOPS) AND TROY

SUNRAY CATCHERS

Today, in the prison chow hall, I overheard a young female officer talking to another officer. She was talking about her special little girl. Seems this little girl was standing on the front seat of her car the other day, grabbing at the sunrays as they reflected off the windshield. When her mother asked her what she was doing, this little girl said she was trying to catch a sunray for her mom as a present. The other officer then asked if this mother got to spend time with her special little girl.

"No, but when my career gets back on track, I'll have more time to spend with her, when she is older," said the young mother.

I wanted to scream and tell that mother to spend every single second she possibly can with her child, but I couldn't. Maybe after you read what follows, you will better understand.

It's the awful truth, as it happened to me. It starts with an unwritten letter—a letter I can never send.

Dear Kent,
As I look at you, I see your hair is nicely combed. I remember the hours and gallons of water we used, trying to

train your hair. It always seemed to have a mind of its own. I can see that scar on your lip hardly shows now, too. We were worried about that. You were such a brave little man when I took you to Dr. Nordquist to get those three stitches in it. I was the one who almost fainted when they started sticking you with that needle. The nurse even made me leave the room.

On the way home, I told you that you could have any treat you wanted, for being sdso brave. You wanted a cup of coffee, "Like big men drink," you said. My five-year –old little brave man, drinking coffee in the Rainbow Restaurant, just like big men. It was our secret; lucky Mom never found out, huh?

You have grown tall and nice looking. Grampa always said you were going to be a big man. Guess what I'm proudest of in you? It's your kindness to all things. When we found out that your little dog, Porkchop, was epileptic, you were so happy that you cried. You had seen Porkchop have fits many times, and were sure he would die. For three years after that, you faithfully gave Porkchop his pill every day.

I remember the day you helped me fix my pickup. We sure got greasy—Mom wouldn't even let us in the house for lunch, but we fooled her. We went to the store and got a pizza, then lipped off to Mom and your two brothers, while eating it, still dirty. Yes, that was fun. We laughed a lot that day. I found out later that you did save a piece of pizza for your little brother; it was our secret too.

I've always been proud of you for so many reasons, Kent. Your silent kindness and strength, your loyalty, your soft hearted and secrets you shared with me. I remember how you *used to lay across my lap with your shirt pulled up, exposing your bare back. I would trace my fingers lightly over your skin; it seemed to almost hypnotize you. I had done it many times when you were a baby, to get you to sleep when you weren't felling good. Guess you never grew out of liking it. I liked it too.*

I remember the day I came to tell you that I was going away for a long time—going to prison. You stood silently, listening with your head bowed and tears in your eyes, asking why. You hugged me and ran up into the woods, to your secret fort, crying. I cried too that day Kent. I was ashamed of myself, and of breaking your heart.

You did write me and send me the colored pictures you drew in school. I had them on my cell wall for years, and yes I bragged about them to my friends. I have lain awake many nights wondering who was teaching you to drive, who was your first girlfriend, and how I would tease you about her, as if I were right there with you. I'm sorry for missing so much of you, Kent.

Love,
Daddy

As I stood looking at my special little boy, in a light gray coffin, I was dressed in bright orange overalls. Prison guards were beside me. I wanted to reach and touch him just once more, but the chains on my wrists wouldn't allow it.

It took a mortician to cover that cut on Kent's lip and get his hair to lay down. I'm so awful sorry for missing the last eight years of Kent's life. If only I could have another chance to be the daddy he wanted me to be—the daddy he deserved.

If I could tickle Kent's back once more, or share some secret with him, or tease him and hold him for just a few minutes. God, I would gladly die for the chance.

Kent was killed when he was crushed under a tractor in an accident near Kelso, Washington. He is buried in Mt. Pleasant Cemetary, near the only tree there. So, if you are ever mear that cemetary, and see a six-foot, five-inch, 270-pound beat-up old man on his knees beside that grave, [praying to God in shame, you will know why.

Hopefully you will better understand why I wish he could have read this letter while he was still alive. There are so many things I should have told him. So much time I should have spent with him.

If you have a special child in your life, please don't, for any reason, miss one single second with that child.Don't let what happened to me happen to you. Those moments are so awfully important.

To the lady officer with the special little sunray catcher—please believe me when I say, "For God's sake, spend every single precious moment with your child now! This could be your last chance, because sometimes very special children don't get any older."

Edwin Allen Lee

EPILOGUE

At the end of a row of cells, in the prison cellblock I live in are two telephones. They are blue phones that the inmates can use to call the free world collect on. I've spent countless hours talking to friends and loved ones on those phones over the past thirty years. Talked on them so much, I actually hated the sight of them.

The lady on the other end of the phone talking to me this day, caught me by surprise.

"Don't you worry about a thing Duke," she said, "I'll protect you. "

I got a lump in my throat, was unable to speak for a few moments and finally managed to say something like,

"What you'd have working for you is a cowardly social retard, Marsha."

"I understand, Duke.," she said. "After thirty years in prison, the world is going to be a shock to you. But, don't worry. I'll have a little apartment for you when you get here and if you give me your sizes, I'll get you some clothes too. Believe me Duke, it won't be so bad and I'm really looking forward to working with you."You have to remember that God loves you, Duke. We all love you, we won't let anything happen to you, Duke; you have my word on that."

I coughed or something, a method I've learned to use

to cover emotion in prison. Fact is, I was crying silently, with tears running down both cheeks and damn near speechless. I mumbled something really intelligent like,

"Yeah Marsha, I'm looking forward to working with you, too, and I wanna get a bulldog!"

"Okay Duke, we'll get a bulldog and I'll even try to find you a 26 year old black coffee pot. Mike tells me you can't operate the new coffee makers!"

Thus started my future. I've spent many hours during my prison career writing. It started out as a hobby, went to a way of expressing emotion and finally ended up being published—all quite accidental.

My intent was never to be a writer. I've always wanted to be a doctor, a surgeon. In fact, for twenty years I threw away everything I wrote out of fear that someone might find it and read it. Writing is a terrifying hobby, if you write from the heart that is.

Your innermost feelings on paper, unchangeable, for everyone to see and dissect. A writer of nonfiction, in reality lays his heart at the reader's feet, to be understood and agreed with or stomped on. I once had no intention of ever being so vulnerable, not even with spoken words. You can't survive in prison showing emotion of any type.

Alone with my typewriter, however, I could tell of things the spoken word wouldn't allow me to verbalize due to emotion. My typewriter is a true friend, it knows all my secrets, weaknesses, and fears. It allows me to speak openly and honestly, even cry, alone in my cell, away from prying eyes.

Now, many people have read the feelings I shared with my typewriter. They will want to meet me, and I'm scared to death to face anyone. I'm an institutionalized old convict who wished only to slip into society unnoticed, who now has some of his writings in a bestseller. Scared? Damn right, I'm scared. So scared, a little 110 pound mother of three has to protect me, and I know it. I wasn't always this way. I had to work damn hard to get this retarded. I was almost normal at one time.

Three of us grew up together, cousins, Gary, Dale, and myself. I had two sisters, Judy and Sandra, but growing up in my generation, sisters didn't count for much. They were tolerated, their boyfriends were punching bags and they could be talked into ironing their brother's clothes on special occasions—for a price that is. Like all big brothers, I loved them very much and do so today.

Gary, Dale and myself, all played football, hockey, and did a little boxing in high school. I was screened and invited to be a member of a group called MENSA, when I was a sophomore. It's for people who have an IQ in the upper 2% of the general population. Today, forty years later, they still have a Proctor retest me every five years or so, (trying to rectify their mistake no doubt). Gary and Dale didn't make it, low IQ'd, as they were (joking). Today, Gary is retired from being the head of the Neurology Department at a hospital in North Dakota. He was a specialist in spinal cord surgery. Dale is a professor at a State University, or I think that's what he is. All I base this on, is my Uncle's report that Dale has a "chair" at the University. And, of course, I'm an institutionalized anti-social convict.

However, there is a bright side to all this. I married my high school sweetheart Sandy, had three boys, Guy, Kent (see Sunray Catcher), and Troy, got a divorce, went to prison, married a beautiful young lady named Sheri (see Love & Rage) and had my only daughter Cissy (see Bombee), went back to prison on a parole violation, got a divorce, married a psychologist named Marianne, had no kids with her, thank God, had my parole violated again and now I'm ready to get out of prison.

'Course, I've got some health problems that have to be addressed. Got scar tissue behind my left eye from a beating I took while boxing. They tell me it's not a real big thing, however, and that surgery will take care of it. Then there's this heart problem. Heart is in good shape, it's the arteries around it that are about plugged. Bypass, is the term used by the doctors.

I've been putting this medical stuff off as long as possible, wanting to get it taken care of at the VA when I get out. Least that's the excuse I offer myself. Fact is, I hate medical procedures,—even getting shots. A person would think a man that has brought so much pain into his own life wouldn't think much about a needle shot. But I do. They still cause me to do some bellyaching.

Then, prison hospitals aren't the best possible place to have surgery (to put it mildly). Time has exhausted my excuses. Either I take care of it now or I'll be saddled with medical problems when I get out. I'm a bit concerned or apprehensive about having surgery.

When compared to the fear I have of walking out into society however, it pales. I can only compare my fear of leaving prison with the panic a person might have of being questioned in front of a large audience, about a subject you know nothing about, with at least half of the audience very outspoken against you.

Frightened of making a fool of myself in front of those I love, fearful people will find out just how socially retarded I really am. Fearful that I won't be able to understand the million changes that have taken place since I left freedom; thus ending up living as a unconfined outsider in the fast world of little plastic cars, digital coffee makers, ATMs and cyber space.

Have to go to Oregon and spend some time for a parole violation. The technical terms used for my violation are:

1. Leaving the state without permission—which is true.

2. Being arrested in another state—which is true, arrested in fact for parole violation in Washington State, on an old warrant, overlooked when I was released from Oregon State.

3. Drinking —which is not true .

There was some beer found in the car I was in, it belonged to my son who was drinking. But, by the time I was told of these violations (three months later), proving I was not drinking would be all but impossible. Fact is, I was on both heart block and blood pressure medications; therefore, alcohol would have rendered me dead! I've learned to not argue with any parole official, so I'll not contest any of the aforementioned violations.

The part of this whole technical violation thing that somewhat scares me is the fact that I felt strangely more comfortable after arrest, in jail, than I had felt during the prior three weeks of freedom. In jail I was back in a world I fully understood, on a bunk I could sleep on, eating foods that didn't give me diarrhea and talking to men I could relate to. I was in my element as much as Gary was in his operating theater or Dale in his "Chair."

I knew in advance everything that would happen in my life two or three weeks ahead of time. I would be served with violation papers and be shipped to Shelton, Washington, the receiving center for the Department of Corrections. There I would see the Parole Board in person, have the actual charges against me read to me, be sanctioned, and sent to Walla Walla, Washington for a given number of months. No real secret about that. It's something that never changes.

Kit Bail, the ex-Catholic nun, who is a Board Chair person, still uses cheap perfume, has bad breath and is no stranger to ring around the collar on the white blouses she always wears. She will, between emissions of several odors, determine my home address for the next given number of months. She is as close to God as anything I'll ever smell on this earth.

From my jail cell young men will constantly seek my advice on matters concerning their legal problems. They are a common lot, poor for the most part. The vast majority have problems with drugs or alcohol and all of them are scared. I'll tell them the little known facts for first-time offenders.

If they have a court-appointed attorney, they have no legal representation, or damn little. Well over 85% of the people in prisons all across America were represented by court-appointed attorneys. That says it all.

I caution them on anything they tell corrections officials on any level, be it guard or counselor. What they say will all be entered into a prison record and be forever used against a person, regardless of how good or honest their intent may be at the time.

I tell them not to abuse their family by exposing them to prison officials any more than necessary; this includes visits. The assumption of complete and total power is a fact of life when dealing with prison officials. They will embarrass your family, disrespect them, confine them during visits and even ask them to disrobe at the slightest hint of their rule infractions, all under the name of security.

I remind them that no matter how nice, understanding or kind any prison official seems; to get the job they have, they've signed a pledge to shoot to kill you or your family, in the name of security, should it be deemed necessary.

Yes, all prison officials too, cooks, doctors, nurses and chaplains. When near prison officials, your family can be exposed to both abuse and death, and I invite anyone to try prove me wrong on this point.

"Institutionalized!" That's exactly the word for men like me. Products of the state's best, taught by example, belief in what we have seen, with a combined memory to equal NCIC (national criminal identification center), of the wrongs committed against us and our families, under the guise of security and sanctioned as equal justice.

Please don't think that I'm a rare case of institutionalization. It happens to everyone who serves over five years, to some degree. The decision making process has been removed from us for periods of time that make us not only socially handicapped, but angry in our forced strangeness.

I have no idea of how to drive a car with cruise control, what a bar code is, and I have never played a video game. Getting money from an ATM seems strange to me. I have no idea of current prices, fashions, trends, nor can I identify any car made in the last twenty years. I have no idea of what size clothes I wear, how to use a VCR, how to open a savings account, establish credit or find employment.

I'll have no more than forty dollars given to me by prison officials the day I leave here, for work clothes and related expenses, they tell me. In plain English, I'm a total social idiot; a sixty year old institutionalized convict mentally crippled by Washington State's rehabilitation program called prison.

Again I must plead, please don't think I'm a poor-me-innocent-type. I put myself in prison and never argued that. I'm filled with another emotion besides the anger I harbor for the prison system. That's shame for the life I've allowed myself to live. George Sewell said,

"Tears are the tax the conscience pays for guilt."

He sure hit the nail on the head, at least for me. The anger I carry for prison is at least equaled by the anger and shame I feel for my own past ignorance. At night alone with my thoughts, I still utter an inaudible groan when a reminder of some haunting past misdeed slips unexpectedly into my nightly reflections. No court, no sadistic prison official, no beating, can cause me the pain my own memory bestows upon me....nightly.

I have a dream. A dream to someday write a best seller, become financially secure and get to know my family again, as a Grandpa this time. If that beyond-belief dream ever comes true, I hope during some nationally televised interview, a well-known commentator asks me what I learned during my prison experience.

At that point, I'll confess to how me and the prison system worked together in making a paranoid social idiot out of an alcoholic MENSA member in the name of rehabilitation. And let me tell you—it wasn't easy. We had to work at it.

Being a baptized and confirmed Lutheran, raised in the 1950s, in a rural environment, and of a bloodline that is 100% Norwegian, I've always known that Catholics were a spooky lot. They wear those black clothes, worship in those big cathedral-like churches and even speak some foreign tongue during services. Yes, they're a spooky bunch for sure.

Lutherans, in my day, wouldn't be caught dead even drinking from the same bottle as a Catholic.

I recall my uncle, (the quietest most sympathetic uncle), telling me in slack-jawed horror when he found out my high school sweetheart was pregnant.

"Do you mean to tell me, you knocked up a gawddamn Catholic? " He stared at me like I had just been convicted of sodomizing Hitler, or some such evil deed.

So, you might understand my reluctance when some old convict friends were trying to talk me into coming to Catholic services, five years ago when I was transferred to the Monroe Industrial Complex (WSR), in Monroe, Washington from Walla Walla (WSP).

"You'll like it, Duke" said Jim Fogle(author of *Drug Store Cowboy*), a staunch heathen, if I ever knew one.

"They don't play head games" said Gary "Goose" Noble, another heathenistic reject, who would invite lightning upon entry to any church.

"It's plain old-time religion," was the word from something that walked upright, slobbered and constantly farted, who went by the name Jim McFarland. He regularly threatened to whip Christ's ass, if his life didn't improve.

To say I was surprised these trusted, respected and loyal friends, were actually going to church, is an understatement. In many ways It confirmed what I had known all along—those Catholics were a spooky lot for sure.

"Aw come on, Duke; they give coffee and cookies every Thursday night. Besides there is a little lady over there named 'Pat' that everyone just falls in love with," was the word from another mentally and morally diseased old friend, Jerry Albers. I gave up and went. The cookies did it.What I found was a group of convicts in the front four rows of that church that would cause any sensible cop to grab iron or his ass in a hurry. Some of them were even singing in the choir!

That night Fogle introduced me to a tiny lady named Pat, who seemed constantly on the move.

"Welcome," she said.

I just came here to get those sick bastards off my back and get free cookies." I told her pointing at Fogle, Mac and Jerry.

Oh, you're not Catholic then." She said smiling.

"No; can't stand Catholics," I said.

"I've heard so much about you, Duke,." Pat told me laughing. I could see all those demented and twisted misfits, looking so innocent in the front four rows watching us talk.

"Yeah, well I got Modoc here with me just in case you Catholics start rattling those beads or something and we gotta fight our way out of this place," I told Pat.

"It's going to take more than Clifton (Modoc's real name), to help you," she said with a wink and a tiny doubled up fist. I'm a lot tougher than I look and I'm Irish too, so watch out!"

Well, here it is four and a half years later and I'm still going to Catholic services. I ain't stickin' around for no bead rattlin', however. Irish (the nickname I call Pat) became a true friend. She has a grace about her that screamed she cared. I constantly tease her about anything or everything and she will haul off and slug me from time to time.

And as bad as I hate to say so, all those sick bastards in the front four rows were right. I joined the crowd of old hardcore cons who loved Pat. She was always there for us when death touched our families, always had a kind word for an angry heart and never forgot to let us know that we mattered.

Irish came to see me today. She was sad. Jim Fogle's mother had passed away. Another friend's lungs were not getting better and all those old hardcore cons in the front four rows that she loved so much were gone, transferred to other institutions or getting ready for release. Finally, after telling me where and how all my friends were, she sadly said,

"Duke, I'm quitting. Things just aren't the same over at WSR without all you guys. I'm still going to work in Prison Ministries, but I need time for myself too....and it's just too hard watching you guys leave."

There was an emotional silence of a few seconds before I could say,

"Hell Irish, it couldn't have come at a better time. Now Fogle, Goose, Mac, Jerry and I, can say we took you out with us!"

"You're right Duke." She said with a little sad smile, "It sure would be nice if all you guys and Father Ross, could come over to my place someday, you know, for a picnic or a party."

"You've got my word on it." I told Irish, trying to cover my own emotion. With that, it was time for her to go, so I walked with her as far as I could. When we parted, I hollered at her saying,

"I'm gonna send that thing I wrote about the repentant hooker to the Archbishop, Irish."

"You better not!" She said with that wannabe tough Irish look of hers. I watched her walk off, tiny and alone in the rain, to the control center, remembering the times I teased her unmercifully, the times she went to the hole to offer hope to my friends, the times she calmed my angry heart and the times she introduced me to one and all, as her token Norwegian Lutheran.

I'm glad it was raining February 16, 1999, at 10:45 a.m. because Norwegian tears don't show in the rain. There are special people who work in prisons, people who do try to make a difference. Rare though they are, I've known one without equal... "Irish" Pat Hoban.

She is one spooky Catholic us old hard cons will always thank God for and, as quiet as it's kept, she is possibly the best rehabilitation tool in the system.

What Marsha Drake is offering to help, is a 270 pound 6 foot five, gray-haired institutionalized old convict. She is going to protect me, and I need her to do just that. Perhaps "Irish" Pat Hoban took a few of the rough edges off me. And maybe my belief in Jesus, or with luck, my writing ability coupled with God and understanding friends like Marsha, maybe ...just maybe...I'll be speaking to people about my co-defendant and myself some day. In the meantime, I'll continue my relationship with Jesus, think positive and continue writing.

After my release, I'll write another book about being free. Perhaps my transition back into society and the emotions I experience doing it will benefit some reader one of these days. I doubt that I will ever stop fighting or exposing my co-defendant, the prison system, as long as I live. I've seen first hand the monsters they create.

I'm a prime example of the social retardation that comes with doing extended periods of time behind bars. I wonder if people will think I'm strange if I buy a root beer popsickle on a hot day and really enjoy myself sucking on the end of it? You know, until it turns the light color of ice on the end? Would they understand a sixty year old kid enjoying a root beer popsickle?

I wonder if people will look at me as odd if I walk into a quiet church for no apparent reason, just to quietly feel the presence of God ... Alone?

I wonder if people will think ill of me for staying home alone at Christmas and Thanksgiving, or if I start to nervously sweat in crowds, or if I stop to pet too many animals or if I get tears in my eyes when I hold a baby. Or if I get up at all hours of the night and open the front door or make a peanut butter & jelly sandwich. If I sleep on the floor for a while instead of on a soft bed. If I can't carry on a conversation about anything except Jesus, writing, or prison. Or if I'm more afraid of getting a hug from a child in front of a crowd than I am of facing an angry convict with a knife, because the hug may make me cry. If I'd rather have a good conversation with an eight year old child than a conversation with any of today's world's leaders. Or if for no outward reason, I quickly leave the room because I fear my own tears?

I wonder if people would understand or even believe the bond I felt in prison, because men have fought over some convict unknowingly sitting in the chair that was designated "Duke's"... Many times? If I told them of the young convicts who call me "Sir"...Out of respect, not fear. Of the criminals who would fight to the death beside me, if I asked them to do so. If I tried to explain how I can walk out on a crowded prison yard, full of killers and hard core criminals, in any prison in Washington or Oregon and have men stand, and offer me their seats, because they know the pain I've survived.

What if I tried to explain the unquestioned loyalty I have for my convict friends, if I tried to tell them that I get my strength and peace of mind from a tiny lady I call "Irish," and I get it by picking on her. Or if I told them the people who cry most when reading my stories, are the toughest convicts I know. What if I told them the reason I'm like this, is because the two things all convicts learn to do really well is cry alone and hide a fractured heart, no matter what. What if I said more than anything on this earth, convicts fear "YOU" seeing our tears or knowing our shame. And, I wonder if I've got the courage to ever let anyone read this, and will they laugh and think I'm insane ... If I do?

Yes ... Guess I'll take the chance of being laughed at. I'll do it because of a feeling I have; a feeling like standing in line next to a big powerfully built man. You know, the one that stands out in a crowd, deep voice and everything? Remember the feeling of just knowing that man was there? No matter what, looking away or not, you could feel the presence of power. If that big man was truly powerful, chances are he had a gentle smile on his face, maybe even laughed a lot and possibly loved teasing everyone around him. I feel that's the God in him and I feel he's in you, the reader.

It's the same way with little children. If you know a little one is in your area, subconsciously you will be more careful, watch where you step, even warn others to be careful. You feel the presence of the child and it's our nature to protect children. To enjoy teasing them too. I feel that's the God in us all.

Yes, something deep inside us feels the presence of another at times. I've heard many people tell of hearing God, of asking God a question and of having their question answered. Someday, I'll be fortunate enough to hear God, but for now, I feel Jesus.

The other day a young mentally handicapped man approached me bashfully in the prison cell block I live in.

"Do ya think I can talk to you sometime when you ain't too busy maybe?," he asked, looking at the floor.

"Sure, I got time right now; what do ya need?" I answered, kind of puzzled.

"The guard wrote me up for not going to the hospital yesterday an' those guys over there said you know how to fix it so they can't put me inna hole," he said pointing to several other inmates watching at a distance, obviously thinking it was funny. They no doubt believed they were playing a cruel joke on the handicapped young man, by sending him up to a crabby old outspoken convict like me.

"Do you want me to file an appeal on your write-up?"

"I don't know what it is, just don't wanna go to the hole," he answered looking at the floor.

"Let me see your write-up," I told him.

He dug deep in two or three pockets finally producing a wrinkled infraction report for failing to go to a hospital appointment. I could smell his breath and he had not showered for a long time.

"How come you didn't go to the hospital?" I asked him.

"Didn't know I was 'sposed to," he answered.

"You have to remember to read the Call Out Sheet, on the bulletin board, I told him as I pointed the bulletin board out to him. He hardly glanced at it, quickly looking back down at the floor... Embarrassed.

"Yeah, I know," he said, "but I can only read my name. I can't read the other stuff."

A cold rush of air entered my solarplexus. The poor kid couldn't even read.

"You wait right here." I told him. Seeing the day-shift sergeant in his office. I took the kid's write-up and went directly to him. The conversation between that sergeant and myself isn't in the vein of this writing, so it's better left unwritten. However, the sergeant did pull up the kid's record on the computer and saw that he was handicapped and was illiterate. He then tore up the kid's write-up. When I returned and told the kid his write-up was gone, he said,

"Now I won't hafta go to the hole?," with a big smile on his face, and walked away.

He didn't say, "Thank you, Duke." He didn't have to. I felt God in that kid's handicap; there's an open rightness about him and his need. Today, whenever I see that kid, I feel a rightness, a need to tease him ... And when I walk away, I silently thank God, through Jesus, for bringing a special person such a good feeling into my life. You know something else? When I think back on the times I felt closest to God, it's the feeling I remember most. Whatever deed proceeded it isn't important in my memory. Hopefully, you will recognize my retardation and not laugh at me if we meet one day. Perhaps you will better understand if I look at the floor too. It's the shame I feel for the memories I've got.

The prison system, with its carefully designed falseness and corrupt failure, didn't start the process that made me what I am today. I did that. They are but a codefendant in the destruction of a careless, young, trusting and gullible mind. The rehabilitation of that mind is left to God, my family and a tiny understanding voice I've heard only over the telephone. Anything positive, anything I create or improve on, from here on out, is due only to the individuals mentioned. If you know an ex-prisoner who is now a contributing member of your family and community, it's due only to those who helped, loved and understood him after release.

The softness in my writing was brought to the surface by a lady I've never even seen, named Donna Bethers. She gave me my first typewriter because my writings made her cry. Lucy Leu's tears gave me strength as she taught me nonviolent communication. "Irish" Pat Hoban, found a long-buried gentleness in me. Nancy San Carlos honors me by courageously allowing me to fight the system with her. Marsha Drake, with her son Mike, reawakened me to the beautiful unconditional love bond between a mother and son, and are rehabilitation to me. My daughter's mother Sheri who will foever have a special palce within my heart—we grew a lot together. And the two little ladies who give me the guts to believe in myself are; Evon Satcher, who gives me confidence, understanding, a future and believes in me wholeheartedly; and of course, my little girl, Cissy, who gives me the highest honor I could ever hope to gain in this life...Her Bombee.

The kindness and understanding of the ladies mentioned above have made me living proof of my belief that rehabilitation by solitary incarceration alone, is like attempting to fight fire with gas. A wise old crippled hero, Franklin Delanor Roosevelt said,

"Human kindness has never weakened the stamina nor softened the fiber of a free people. A nation does not have to be cruel in order to be tough."

CONCRETE HELL
by LEO DOBBS

while he was in
Solitary Confinement

PLEASE PROTECT US LORD,

FOR WE ARE SO ALONE.

PEOPLE IN A DREAM WORLD,

ALL OUR OWN.

PEOPLE SO CALM

AND AT EASE IT SEEMS,

BUT WHO ARE HAUNTED EACH NIGHT

BY OUR PAST DREAMS.

YOU KNOW US LORD,

YES, YOU KNOW US WELL.

FOR WE CRY IN PRAYER,

FROM THIS CONCRETE HELL.

Messages From the Heart
Book Requests and Orders

Single copies of *Messages from the Heart* may be purchased for $14.95, which includes the cost of shipping and handling ($10.95 plus $4.00 shipping). A portion of the proceeds from the book sales will be donated to S.H.I.P, an organization dedicated to helping the handicapped in prisons across the nation. Send your payment by check or money order payable to:

Wino Publishing
C/o George Kolin
P.O. Box 147
Washougal, WA 98642

Author's Warning:
Wino Publishing and/or Edwin Allen Lee has no connection with Teri Taylor Publishing or Angel Tears and is in no way responsible for their actions.

About the Author

In 1961, Edwin Allen Lee was invited into MENSA (a group considered to be among the most intelligent 2% in the USA) and has been a member for over 39 years. Today, he holds a Bachelor of Arts degree (BA) in Inter-disciplinary Studies with an Associates degree in Business and Psychology, which he earned while in prison. He is a member of Toastmasters International. He was also a professional heavyweight boxer with a 10 and 1 record.

Edwin Allen Lee writings have appeared in *Reader's Digest* and he has also been published by *Bantam Books*. In 1998, he won *The American Pen Award* for his story, "*Stranger behind Glass*," and in 1999, the *Amelia Award* for his short story, "*Guilt Free*." Over 4000 stories were submitted to the recently published, *Chicken Soup for the Prisoner's Soul*. Out of the 101 stories that were finally selected, 5 of them were written by Edward Allen Lee.

Edwin Allen Lee recently appeared on national television on *48 Hours* as a spokesperson for the transitional release of inmates. He has been a facilitator in the *Alternatives to Violence Program* and *Nonviolent Communications(NVC)*, as well as *The Breaking the Barrier's Program* at other correctional facilities while in prison. But Nancy Carlos' *S.H.I.P.* program for helping disabled and disadvantaged prisoners and *The Seattle Millionaires Club* for helping the homeless are the two programs Edwin is the proudest to be a member of.

Printed in the United States
6398

9 780759 640627